Back to Life:

Love After Heartbreak

Back to Life:

Love After Heartbreak

Shantaé

www.urbanbooks.net

Urban Books, LLC
300 Farmingdale Road, NY-Route 109
Farmingdale, NY 11735

Back to Life: Love After Heartbreak

ISBN 13: 978-1-945855-79-5
ISBN 10: 1-945855-79-7

First Mass Market Printing November 2018
First Trade Paperback Printing June 2018
Printed in the United States of America

10 9 8 7 6 5 4 3 2 1

This is a work of fiction. Any references or similarities to actual events, real people, living or dead, or to real locales are intended to give the novel a sense of reality. Any similarity in other names, characters, places, and incidents is entirely coincidental.

Distributed by Kensington Publishing Corp.
Submit orders to:
Customer Service
400 Hahn Road
Westminster, MD 21157-4627
Phone: 1-800-733-3000
Fax: 1-800-659-243

Back to Life:

Love After Heartbreak

Shantaé

Chapter 1

Dakota "Kota" Bibbs

To New Beginnings

I sat at the edge of my bed, my hands gripping the mattress on both sides of me. My eyes were cast down to the plush white carpet. I could only shake my head in disbelief, thinking, *how did I not see this coming? Shouldn't I know by now that his words are too good to be true? Like, I really shouldn't be shocked right now, but I am.*

Like a fool, I'd fallen for the okey-doke once again. Was so used to being taken for granted and used that it no longer hurt. I was past pain at this stage, and surprisingly my tear ducts were dry, unable to release a single drop. That was how I knew that this was it and my relationship was officially over. I'd done my fair share of crying behind this man, and I'd had enough. I was so calm that Breelyn, who I had on speaker-phone, kept asking if I was sure I was okay. She was used to the hell-raising, shit-talking Kota, but right now I just didn't have the energy to do all that.

"Kota, maybe he just got caught up with the kids. I'm sure there's a perfectly good expla-nation for why he didn't show up," my cousin offered, not because she believed what she was saying but because she wanted to make me feel better. She was still out of town but called this morning to see how things had gone last night only for me to inform her that I'd been stood up.

"You and I both know that ain't what the deal is. Besides, I was so desperate thinking the nigga was somewhere fucked up or dead that I broke down and called David to ask him if Tell was still with him. Was thinking maybe they'd gone overboard with the celebrating or something. Imagine my surprise when he asked me what the hell I was talking about. Didn't even know his cousin was getting out yesterday and surely didn't pick him up. And best believe that fuck nigga was all too happy to share that li'l info with me. Can't stand his ho ass." I laughed sarcastically.

"Damn, I'm sorry, Kota," was all she said in response before going mute.

Knew she was just itching to ask me about her funky-ass ex, but she refrained. There was a time and a place for everything, and this here conversation was about me and my piece-of-shit nigga, not hers. "Don't be sorry. Should've known better. Montell came out the gate letting me know what it's about to be. All that shit he's been talking since he's been away. All lies. Ain't a damn thing changed," I spoke low.

"If you need to get away, you could always come visit me for a few days. I miss you like crazy, mama."

"Damn, you don't know how much I wish I could come down. I miss you too, but I just came off a month-long break, and business is crazy for me right now. Guess I'll just have to wait until you make it back this way in a few months. Still can't believe you left me like that," I pouted.

"Some days I can't believe it either, but no worries. The dynamic duo will be back together before you know it," she said, and I laughed. We talked for another hour or so before promising to talk at the same time the following day like we'd done daily since she left.

In every other aspect of my life, I was sharp and strong-minded, and I took no shit, but when it came down to my love life, and this one nigga in particular, I was stupid and obviously too forgiving. It was clear that my so-called man was aware of that as well. That much was evident by the untouched comforter and fluffed pillows on his side of our king-sized bed. Somehow I fell asleep waiting up for him last night and awoke this morning to find that he hadn't bothered coming home at all.

Before passing out, I recalled blowing up Montell's phone for hours while I sipped on a bottle or two of Belaire Rosé. Had no idea where he was, but my mind had been consumed with various reasons or situations that could have kept him from coming home to me after being gone for so long. How could my face not be the first he wanted to see when he got out? Figured that something bad must have happened to him. You know how you go from worried for their welfare to angry, thinking he was on some fuck shit, then all the way back to worrying again? My head pounded just thinking about it. No, that ache was probably due to the excessive amount of bubbly I'd consumed the night before, but whatever.

Finally, I got up to dispose of the meal I'd prepared for us yesterday evening that now sat cold and untouched at the dinner table. "Un-fucking-believable," I said as I gazed over the extravagant spread that was before me. I'd done my thing just like Sylvia Bibbs had taught me. All his favorites were prepared just the way he liked. Went all out for my man only for him to shit on me like he'd been doing throughout the duration of our relationship.

Two outside babies, multiple incarcerations, and on top of all that, the nigga couldn't seem to keep his hands to himself. If all that wasn't enough to tear me away from him, the mediocre sex should have been the straw that broke the camel's lumpy-ass back. Many times when women put up with a lot of bullshit from their man, it's because the dick is bomb and we can't see ourselves giving that up to the next female. Believe it or not, really good sex is hard to come by. We'll tolerate a lot of shit behind some good pipe. At least I knew I would, but that was absolutely not the case with Montell Mathis. And I loved sex, so this was a really big deal for me.

I went all out in the bedroom to please my man, and I expected the same effort in return. He had a nice size on him and everything, but the baby had absolutely no clue what to do with it. When I tried to talk to him about our sex life, he took it the wrong way, and that was the first time one of our arguments turned physical, with him passing the first lick. My mouth was somewhat reckless, so I thought maybe I'd approached the conversation the wrong way. Feeling like I'd insulted him and bruised his ego, I forgave him for reacting the way he did. Sadly, that wasn't the last physical altercation we had. It was only the beginning of a violent cycle between us.

Like I said, I was a smart chick, hood and book educated, but for the life of me, I could not shake this man. Couldn't figure out what it was about him that made me think it was okay to settle for less. I'd met Montell a little over four years ago through my cousin Breelyn. At the time, she was dating Montell's cousin David, and that nigga there wasn't worth a fucking nickel and treated Breelyn terribly. He was so bad that at one point he had her living in the same home with his baby mama and son like that was the thing to do. Seriously, they had the whole *Sister Wives* thing going on over there. And he had a problem with his hands as well. I was thinking that abusing women was something that ran in the family or something.

So, yeah, when Montell first approached me, talking about, "Can I take you out?" I was like, "No way," and turned his ass down without hesitation. I mean, you know what they say: birds of a feather or whatever. He and David were thick as thieves, so I assumed that he was just as foolish as his family. Not deterred in the least, Montell continued to pursue me, and in the end, his persistence paid off. He was so sweet and attentive that I fell for his handsome ass hard and fast. So much so that I ignored the signs that told me early on that he simply wasn't the man for me. Trust, the red flags were popping up all over the damn place.

A mere eight months into our relationship, both Montell and I were tagged in a post on Facebook by some ratchet claiming to be carrying his baby. Bitch said she was already six months pregnant, so if that was true, it would mean that this nigga had been cheating for damn near our entire relationship and I hadn't a clue. Hell, the way she was popping shit on the 'book, I was confused about who of the two of us was the side chick. Let her tell it, Montell was her man, and I was the home-wrecker.

Of course, he denied it, claiming that folk just didn't want to see us together and that this was all the result of bitches hating on us. Yeah, fucking right, bruh. By this time, he'd already shown his true colors, so there wasn't shit that spectacular about our relationship for anyone to hate on. Montell hardly worked, and he sucked at hustling, which led to him being in and out of jail. In other words, he didn't contribute much to our household. Like being fine as fuck was all this man had going for him.

Despite the gut feeling I had, I gave my baby the benefit of the doubt. A little over three months after ol' girl posted that shit on social media, the baby was born, and a DNA test proved beyond a shadow of a doubt that he was indeed the father of Ho-esha's baby girl. Her name was actually Ayesha, but I didn't give a fuck. I called it like I saw it. At first, my issue was with my man because he was the one I was committed to, but this girl went out of her way to harass and fuck with me. So, after all the drama she brought to my life, I wanted my round with her rat ass. So many times I wanted to bust a cap in her ass but refrained because of their daughter. Even after all this mess and another baby with an entirely different female, I stayed. I already knew I should have left his ass right then, but I didn't. I don't know if it was the fear of being all alone again or if it was because of how much I loved him. Maybe I just didn't want Ho-esha's ass to have him. Whatever it was, it was an unhealthy situation for all parties involved.

Prior to getting with Montell, I had been single for two years. I fucked around with, like, two dudes in between, but neither situation was serious. Before that, I had been in a relationship with my high school sweetheart until he joined the Navy when we were both nineteen years old. Over the course of the first six months following his departure, things quickly fell apart between us. The distance was too much, and since I'd declined his proposal of marriage and an opportunity to join him and live on base as his wife, he didn't see the point in continuing our relationship. I loved him, but at the time I felt we were much too young to even be considering marriage. I was heartbroken but eventually moved past it. Or at least I thought I did.

A few months later I ran into him, and all those old feelings came flooding back. I was prepared to act on them until he told me he'd recently gotten married to a chick he met in Maryland and they were expecting their first child together. I'd fucked around and missed my chance of marrying my true love, and I was devastated. The happiness in his eyes and the elation in his voice when he spoke of his wife crushed me. He was in love with this woman only months after dumping me, and that fucked my head up. It was like I suddenly realized that I wanted her life. Her happiness. Her man. Didn't matter to me how young I was anymore. I now wanted what he wanted, but it was too late for us.

So, in the end, I settled for Montell. Longing for love and a committed relationship, my loneliness and broken heart led me to giving in to a fuck boy when I should have kept it moving until I met the man I was meant for. Now here I was sitting in my three-bedroom, two-and-a-half-bath home all alone. No children and now no man to love me and fill my lonely days and nights. I was doing what I loved for a living and also helping others do the same, as an author with my very own publishing company. I had enough money to do all the things that made me happy, and I had an amazing family to love on me. Still, I had no one worthwhile by my side as my life partner to share all of that with. All this time I'd been trying to turn Montell into that person, but it just wasn't in him.

He was released from Lew Sterrett yesterday after serving six months on some dumb shit. The entire time he was there he swore up and down that when he got out things between us would be different. This wasn't the first time he'd made jailhouse promises like this when he was locked up, but for some reason, I trusted his words this time. He was going to put forth a real effort to find gainful employment. His children would become a priority, and he would spend more time with them. All the fighting on me was a thing of the past, and these bitches would no longer come between us because I was all he wanted and needed.

If that were the case, where the fuck was he?

He refused to let me come pick him up, claiming David would drop him off at the house right after he took him to see his children. At the time I thought, *cool, he's already keeping one of his promises by making more of an effort where his children are concerned.* Couldn't respect a man who didn't handle his responsibilities with his babies. Now, here it was damn near twenty-four hours after he got out and I had yet to hear from him or see his face. He was well aware of the plans I made for us, but he didn't respect me or care enough about my feelings to even call, let alone come home.

I'd said it dozens of times before, but I was done with this shit. Done with giving this nigga my hard-earned money only for him to turn around and give it to one of his baby mamas or spend it on the loud that he smoked all day every day while I busted my ass getting my coins. Tired of letting this nigga drop me off at my office only for him to pick me up an hour after I told him to be there, with an empty tank of gas. I mean, damn, if you were gon' disrespect a bitch by running your hoes and homeboys around in my shit all day, the least you could do was ask them mu'fuckas to toss you a few dollars on the petrol.

I was also tired of having to fight like I was still living in Highland Hills, banging with the jealous hoes who had it out for me. Truthfully, I was giving it just as good as I got it. Yeah, that nigga put his hands on me, but that didn't mean he was just kicking my ass. Most times he was more busted up than I was at the end of our fights, because I was not a punk at all. My hands were official because Elijah Raheem made sure Breelyn and I could handle ourselves. Just ask Montell. He was well aware of the power behind my jab and right hook.

Lastly, I was so damn tired of not being satisfied sexually. I honestly thought that was what pissed me off the most. I'd been true to this man for years. Niggas constantly coming at me and being turned down all for a man who wasn't even fucking me properly. Where they do that at? Being loyal to a pussy nigga was no longer part of my pedigree after today. There was no excuse or a way to come back from the way he played me last night. Again, I'd said it many times before, but in my heart of hearts, I knew I was really done this time.

Y'all don't have to believe me, though. I can show you better than I can tell you. Come take a ride with me and get acquainted with the new and improved Dakota Layne Bibbs aka Kota B.

"To new beginnings," I said out loud before downing the rest of the flat champagne.

Chapter 2

Breelyn "Greedy" Waiters

A Woman in Distress

"Oh my God, what are you doing? Let . . . me . . . gooo," I slurred while trying but failing to snatch away from the man who was attempting to place me in the back seat of a new-model Lexus.

I was completely wasted, and now some lame was trying to take me home with him to do God knows what to me. Knew better than to drink as much as I did but I needed something, anything, to make me feel better or possibly give me temporary amnesia. After I talked to Kota, David had been on my mind all damn day, and I wanted to erase him from memory if only for a little while. It actually worked, but by trying to drink thoughts of him away, I found myself drunk off my ass with the possibility of being raped or worse in the near future.

"Come on, little lady. My buddy and I just want to show you a good time. Don't you want to have a good time?" he whispered in my ear nastily, sounding like the pervert he was.

I guessed he thought that shit sounded sexy, but even in my drunken state it wasn't. His voice and rank breath made my skin crawl. I'd fucked up in the worst way, and I was about to pay for my mistake. Seeing double and feeling sick to my stomach, I knew there was no way I could fight off one let alone two men at once, but I was determined to try.

I continued to struggle with the more aggressive guy while his friend peeped the scene, seeming unsure if he wanted to participate in what his boy had in mind. Although intoxicated, I could see the uncertainty in his eyes. "Please," I cried drunkenly, turning my attention to him right as his friend tried closing the door with one of my legs still hanging out of the car. He looked like he was about to give in to me when a deep voice boomed from nearby.

"Aye, man, what the fuck y'all doing to that girl?" the stranger asked in an aggressive tone. I could barely make out his face due to my rapid blinking and blurry vision, but his voice told me he played no games.

"We were just giving her a ride home," the guy who was manhandling me lied nervously as he eyed the gun the man had at his side.

"Don't look to me like she want a ride from your ass. Is this what mu'fuckas doing nowadays? Preying on drunk females and taking advantage of 'em?" he asked, pulling the door open and snatching me from the back seat like I weighed nothing.

"Honestly, bro, we were really just giving her a ride." The guy continued to plead his case as my knight in shining armor whisked me away.

"Nigga, shut'cho lying ass up with that 'bro' shit. I should pop both you punk muthafuckas," he spat over his shoulder before pulling me farther away from my would-be attackers. "Did you drive here?" he asked, looking me over with concern.

"Umm, I . . . No," I stammered, looking around the lot. *Did I drive? No, I took an Uber, I think.* I barely knew where I was at that point, and my jumbled thoughts only seemed to heighten my anxiety and nausea. "I don't know," I whined in a childlike voice.

"Fuck, man! Yo' ass don't even know if you drove? You're way too beautiful to be out here like this, baby girl," the stranger said, shaking his head at me.

The look on his face told me how pitiful I was looking right about now, and that made me sad for some reason. Pulling away from him, I took off in the other direction with tears clouding my vision. I would just have to find my way home on my own. I didn't want anyone feeling sorry for me, especially him. I was thankful that he was there to get me out of that sticky situation, but I no longer wanted or needed to be in his presence. My wobbly-ass legs and distorted vision were telling an entirely different story, however. I didn't need to be out here like this by myself. The other two men weren't able to do what they wanted to do to me but someone else surely would if I kept this up. Anyone with eyes could tell I was way past my limit. My body was swaying, and my feet were beginning to feel extra heavy.

"Yo, where the fuck you think you going, ma?" my rescuer said, quickly catching up with me. When dude turned me around to face him, I could no longer hold in the contents of my upset stomach. The sudden jerking movement messed me up, causing me to empty everything I'd eaten today onto the ground with a good amount landing on myself as well as his nice sneakers.

Shaking his head and cursing under his breath, he turned his head up to the sky and looked to be asking the Lord for the strength not to snap my neck. I felt horrible for destroying his shoes, but I did feel a little less drunk all of a sudden. My savior gave me a death stare but still grabbed my hand, leading me back in the direction I had just come from. When we reached his nice Suburban truck, he went to the back to let the hatch up and seemed to be searching for something. I knew there was no way I could get in this nice truck with my soiled clothing, so right there in the brightly lit parking lot, I removed my white V-neck tee and my favorite boyfriend jeans along with my white chucks, which were now ruined.

"Girl, what the fuck you doing?" he shrieked when his eyes landed on me. I was standing there with my forehead against the passenger's window wearing nothing but my matching bra and panty set. The undergarments matched my skin so closely that if you weren't close enough to me, it might seem that I was out here in my birthday suit. The lace material gave a nice outline of my cinnamon-colored nipples, and my ass was hanging out of the panties, but I was too out of it to give a damn.

He dipped his head back in the truck and quickly came out with a shirt that he placed over my head and down my body, not bothering to put my arms through the sleeves. I supposed his main focus was covering me up, while his eyes darted around the lot making sure no one besides him had seen me half naked. My clothing he then placed in a plastic bag and tossed inside his whip. His Jordans were now on the ground next to my Chucks, and he wore a pair of Nike slides. After opening the passenger door, he placed me inside and leaned over me to strap me in my seat belt. His hair smelled so damn good that my drunk butt sniffed the top of his head, inhaling the scent all loud like a big kid.

Chuckling lightly, he ran his hand over his 360-degree waves before closing the door and walking around to the driver's side. Once he was inside the car, I recall him asking me where I lived. I knew the answer, but for some reason, I was having a difficult time giving him the details. Was starting to feel like I was tripping off more than just alcohol. I wasn't a heavy drinker at all, but I could normally hold my liquor a little better than this. In the midst of my rambling thoughts, I could hear my Superman mumbling and cursing under his breath, asking himself what the fuck he was going to do with me and how I'd gotten in the way of some job he was supposed to have completed tonight. His one-

sided shit talking was all I remembered before
his voice faded and everything went black.

Mortified summed up how I felt waking up in
a strange man's bed in an extended-stay hotel
room wearing what I assumed was one of his
T-shirts. My mind was still cloudy, but I did
remember bits and pieces from the night before,
his scent being one of them. It was something
I could never forget because I had been sur-
rounded and consumed by it as I slept. What I
didn't recall was how good-looking the man was
who had rescued me. Those beautiful lips, the
bottom more pink and the upper one brown and
closer to his honey skin tone. Jaw line strong,
with thick eyebrows and tight brown eyes that
were so dark they looked coal black with curly
lashes. Even the thick scar between his eyes was
cute. Early morning waves popping just like
they had been the night before. He was ruggedly
handsome and far from a pretty boy. Couldn't
describe him as a thug, either. He was just . . .
different. Mysterious even. But definitely fine.

Closing my eyes, I cringed as I caught a flash-
back of me trying to put the pussy on him in my
drunken state and being turned down. That's
how I ended up in the bed alone with him taking
the couch. How embarrassing. Now I was lying

here watching him as he stood in his in-suite kitchen, shirtless, cooking breakfast. He was wearing jeans that hung low, giving me a perfect view of the tight-ass six pack and sexy V-cut leading down into his True's. From what I could see, his lovely body was unblemished, free of tattoos or piercings.

"So, are you going to sit there and stare all morning, or are you going to come put something in your stomach?" he asked, turning to face me wearing a blank expression.

My face flushed red in embarrassment at being caught ogling him. "I'm not really hungry. I should probably get going anyhow," I said, finally rising from the bed with a long stretch. Eyes closed, hands raised above my head, unaware that he was still watching me. I was too busy thinking about how good his shirt smelled. Was definitely taking it home with me.

Upon opening my eyes, I found his dark ones on me, traveling up and down my body, causing me to quickly lower my arms. Just that fast, I forgot that all I was wearing was a T-shirt, so I'd just given him a good look at the lower half of my naked body. It wasn't like he hadn't seen my goodies already. If I remembered correctly, he'd bathed me the night before, so I was sure he'd already gotten an eyeful.

He cleared his throat before speaking. "Come on. The least you can do is have breakfast with me after what you put me through last night. When we're done I'll take you wherever you need to go," he said with a quick shake of his head before turning back to the stove to flip the last pancake.

"Okay," I mumbled timidly, walking over to the dining area. After placing everything on the table, he grabbed my hand and blessed the food. He had pancakes, turkey bacon, hash browns, cheese eggs, and grits. I loved to eat, so I wasted no time digging in, piling my plate up just as high as his. He chuckled in amusement as he watched me go ham on my three fluffy pancakes. I had no shame in my game when it came to my vittles. That's how I earned the nickname Greedy from my brother, Rah. Didn't play games trying to be cute as I ate, either. I could really put it away, and my host seemed to think it was funny. "So tell me, how much of a fool did I make of myself last night?" I asked between bites of food while he continued to gawk at me.

"You mean besides you trying to molest me then cussing me out when I refused to give you the dick?" he teased, causing me to pause mid-chew.

"Yeah, besides that?" I asked matter-of-factly, pretending to not be embarrassed. Inside, though, I was so ashamed.

He smiled brightly with a nod before answering, "You didn't necessarily make a fool of yourself, but you did put yourself in a fucked-up position. Those geeky bastards may have looked normal on the outside, but they had ill intentions where you were concerned. You tried your best to fight them off, but you were way too intoxicated. Shouldn't drink like that when you go out alone," he advised like he was telling me something I didn't already know.

"I know, but I really feel like somebody slipped me something. There have been occasions where I drank way more than that and I was still able to function, but last night it seemed like I was outside my body or some'n. I still should have known better, because I was already in a jacked-up headspace before I even left my place to hit the bar. I wouldn't have seen it coming if someone did do something like that, so thank you for helping me out and not turning away from what was happening," I told him, truly grateful that he had come to my aid.

"You're welcome. I ain't the type of man to turn a blind eye to shit like that. If it had been my mother or if I had a sister I would want someone to look out for them the same way I did for you," he said. I nodded my understanding.

"You don't have to answer if you don't want to, but who is David?" he asked, surprising the hell out of me.

"How—"

"You called out for him in your sleep," he answered before I could even get my question out.

"He's my ex and also the reason I was there last night trying to drink away my sorrows," I admitted, dropping my head.

"Hold ya head up, ma. It'll get better," he offered sincerely while lifting my face back up by my chin.

I felt electricity and warmth shoot through me at the feel of his hands on my skin. He had to have felt it as well, because he pulled his hand away from me like he had touched something hot, but he continued looking into my eyes. He didn't know me, so he had no idea that I had been hiding out in Jacksonville for almost a year and was still in agony over a man who couldn't care less about me. "When? When will it get better?" I wanted to scream at him. From his expression, I could tell he wanted me to elaborate on my situation with David, but he didn't press any further.

"Since you ruined your clothes last night I went out to Walmart this morning to pick you up a few things. I guessed on the sizes, so forgive me if what I have for you is too big or too small. I already showered, so the bathroom is yours," he said before standing to collect our plates.

"No, let me," I said, touching his arm lightly. There was that damn sensation again. Never in my life had I felt anything like it.

He looked down at my hand before bringing his eyes up to meet mine. Boldly, I wrapped my small hand around his wrist, and damn if I didn't feel this strong-ass connection with him in that moment. Gazes still locked, it was like he could see right through me and I him. Like he had the power to take away all the bad and all the pain only to replace it with love and good memories. I was doing the absolute most right now making something as simple as a good guy looking out for a helpless woman more than what it was, clearly romanticizing his kind gesture. Snapping out of the trance, I removed my hand before speaking.

"Doing the dishes is the least I can do for all that you've done for me." He didn't protest but continued to watch me as I took on the task of washing the dishes and cleaning the small mess he'd created while cooking. "Hey, I recall you saying something about a job you were supposed to do last night. Sorry that I got in the way of that," I apologized.

His eyes widened in surprise before recovering. Probably didn't think I would remember anything from last night. "It's cool. I was able to handle it once I got you in bed," he replied.

This time it was me who wanted him to elaborate. My nosy ass wanted to know exactly what his job was and why he would be doing it at that time of night, in a bar for that matter, but he didn't speak on it, so I continued scrubbing the pan. When I was done, I headed to the bathroom, where he said my things would be. It was so crazy to me that I didn't want to leave him just yet. I attributed it to being depressed and lonely for so long.

An hour later we pulled up to my apartment complex, and we both kind of just sat there not knowing what to say but not quite ready to part ways. Looking out of the window I was relieved to see my black Dodge Challenger in its designated spot. Was scared I left it in the parking lot of the bar, but clearly, I'd taken an Uber there. I chuckled to myself when a thought came to mind.

"What's so funny?" he asked, looking my way.

"It's funny that after last night and this morning I still have no clue what your name is. How crazy is it that I'm just now asking?" I laughed, and so did he.

"DeMario, but people call me Rio," he told me.

"DeMario. I like that." I smiled to myself. His accent reminded me of a New Yorker, but I didn't want to assume or get in his business.

"Thank you, Breelyn," he said with a smile. "You told me your name in the car last night," he said in response to the surprised look on my face.

"Oh, well, um, thanks again for everything. Guess I'll see you around." I shrugged as I reluctantly removed myself from his ride. Who was I kidding? The man was laid up in a hotel, so it was obvious that he wasn't from around here. I realized that the likelihood of us seeing one another again was slim to none, and the farther I got from his car, the more that depressed feeling I'd become accustomed to inched its way to the surface.

DeMario. The kind savage. His eyes held his truth. Fine as hell and compassionate but would still fuck shit up when necessary. He was just the type of man who could take my mind off David, but I wouldn't get a chance to find that out. "Oh well, guess I'll have to get over his ass myself," I mumbled as I closed and locked the door to my cozy little apartment.

The sparsely decorated space had been home for the last nine months. The only rooms I went all out with the décor for were my bedroom and personal bathroom. Wasn't really concerned about the rest of the place, but it was a must that I be comfortable and feel at home in those two rooms. Wasn't like I had friends or people who visited me on the regular, and I didn't plan to be in town much longer anyhow. I was missing my family like crazy, especially Kota. We'd never spent this much time apart, and it was killing me not being able to see my best friend every day. Was starting to realize that running away from my problems may not have been the best way to handle things.

Since I'd already showered and had a hearty breakfast, I planned to spend the rest of the day clocking some z's in my plush, queen bed.

Knock. Knock. Knock.

I heard the door as I stood in the kitchen taking a second bottle of water to the head. My butt was still dehydrated from drinking like a fool last night. I didn't move toward the front to open it until I finished off the whole bottle. Thinking it was just my nosy neighbor, Jess, wondering why I hadn't come home last night, I snatched the door open without checking, only to find DeMario standing there. For a moment we didn't speak. Eyes roaming up and down one another, his breathing pattern matching mine. Rapid and heavy. The longing in his eyes spoke to the want and need in my heart. I'd wanted to kiss him and suck on that bottom lip since I woke up this morning and saw his face, so that's exactly what I did. Stepped up, lovingly cupped his face, and connected my lips to his, like kissing strange men was something I did on the regular. I thought I shocked the shit out of him, because it took a few seconds for him to join in on the kiss. Boy when he did, it was on! I didn't know this man from Adam, but his tongue was magic, and I craved more. And, baby, when I say this man gave me more, he gave in a way that I'd never experienced in my life. That single kiss was the beginning of something spectacular.

Chapter 3

Dakota

Bouncing Back

Three months. That's how long it had been since I got rid of Montell's tired ass, and I must admit I was feeling more and more like the old Kota B every day. My glow up, comeback, or whatever the hell you want to call it was way too real. I'd been going out more, done lost about fifteen pounds, and my family and I were back tight like we used to be.

See, my people didn't care too much for Montell because of the way he treated me, so it caused me to distance myself from them. I hated going around them because I was so ashamed of the fool I'd become, and I didn't want to be judged by anyone. How could I not be ashamed after receiving a call from my daddy one afternoon saying that, as he and my uncle were leaving the barbershop in South Dallas, he'd spotted Montell getting out of my car with a pregnant female? Pops rolled up on Montell, whooped his ass, then took my keys from him, leaving him and his female companion to get to their destination on feet. My gossiping-ass Uncle Herb couldn't wait to tell the family about that shit.

No one could figure out what type of hold dude had on me. Hell, I didn't know myself, but trust and believe me when I say they were all ecstatic that I had finally come to my senses and left him alone. I was too because I'd missed being around them. We were a tight-knit group so not being able to see them or talk to them every day was extremely hard on me. When I was with Montell and I was going through it, I had no one to call and talk to about it because they didn't want to hear it. No one but Breelyn, but she was going through her own thing with David, so I let her be for the most part.

I stayed with Montell after my father beat him up, so even he was fed up. That was hard for me, because my father was one of my best friends and I couldn't even talk to him about my relationship. Told me the only time he wanted to hear Tell's name from my mouth during a conversation between us was when I needed his help getting the mooching-ass nigga out of my house.

That's exactly what happened the day that I decided I was done. Called my people up and told them I was ready to move on, and soon my home was buzzing with cousins, aunts, uncles, and my parents as they assisted me in packing up his shit. We cooked and hung out like it was a damn going-away party without the guest of honor being present. The following day I had a delivery company drop everything off at his mama's house, and I didn't even feel bad about it. If I knew where Ho-esha stayed, I would have sent that shit over there because that's probably where he was hiding out. His other baby mama didn't fuck with him like that, so I knew he wasn't at her house. She was the pregnant woman he was with when my dad rolled up on him that day, and she was done with him after that fiasco. Somehow she got my number from Tell's phone and called me up to apologize. I believed her when she said she had no clue he was in a relationship and promised that whatever they had was over. I felt bad for her because I could tell she was really feeling Montell's lying ass and he'd fucked her over just like he did me.

While browsing through my oversized closet, looking for something comfortable to wear to my parents' home for Sunday dinner, I was interrupted by the ringing of my doorbell. After grabbing a champagne-colored romper from the hanger, I immediately picked my .22 up off the shelf in the closet and went to my home office to check the video.

A bitch had to upgrade security around here after I cut Montell off because he continued to act a fool. I discovered that just because I was done with him, it didn't necessarily mean he was done with me. Tripped me out because I didn't get this much attention from him when we were living under the same roof. I now had to park my cars in the garage because he'd flattened the tires to my Range Rover and the Audi S5 coupe multiple times. Threw rocks and busted out my front bay window when he came home two days after getting out of jail only to discover that I'd changed the locks on him. *So you mean to tell me you get out of jail forty-eight hours prior and you're just now showing your face, but you're somehow surprised that you no longer have access to my home? Yeah, okay, crazy-ass nigga.*

And I stayed strapped ever since the day his stalking ass caught me slipping after work when

I stopped to check the mailbox before pulling into the garage. He got himself together real quick when I pulled my stun gun from my purse and aimed it at him as he begged me to give our love another try. Talking about he didn't have anywhere else to go. All I wanted to know was what the fuck that had to do with me. I'd come to realize that Montell didn't really love or want me. He liked what I could do for him. Knowing that I was no longer going to be his financier had him in his feelings.

Instead of Montell on the screen, I saw my cousin Breelyn looking into the camera and sticking her tongue out at me. I was so happy her silly ass was back in town. Her situation with her ex was very similar to mine, but in her words, she wasn't as strong as I was. In order for her to break free of David's bullshit, she felt she had to flee Dallas altogether. In her mind, distance and time were the keys to breaking the hold he had on her. That was bullshit because she was gone for an entire year, and since she'd touched down, her ass had been ducking the nigga. We all kept telling her that she needed to stop running and stand up to him, but she was too afraid. Hell, she wouldn't even hit the club with me for fear of running into him. I was a fool for Montell when we were together, but I wasn't about to let that man punk me. I stayed beating the streets up just wishing his ass would run up on me so that I could lay him the fuck out. I was a hothead like that, but my cousin, on the other hand, avoided conflict as much as she could.

"Hey, chica." I smiled, opening the door for my favorite girl. Bree and I were close, born only days apart. She was born first, on January 22, and I was born on the twenty-fifth. She was my Aquarius sister, my rider and heart. Same middle names and all. From birth, we'd been the best of friends and celebrated our birthdays together every year as far back as I could remember. Only missed last year because she was away, and in her absence, I found it difficult to function or get excited on my big day. I ended up having dinner with Rah and calling it a night. He tried his best to cheer me up and shower me with gifts, but I was missing my bestie in the worst way. Was too glad to have her back by my side. Over the last year, we'd FaceTimed a lot and texted one another nonstop, but there was nothing like having her here with me in the flesh.

"Hey, mama," she replied as we embraced. "I should have known your slow butt wouldn't be ready when I got here," she complained as she waltzed past me with her overnight bag. She looked amazing in a floral-print, long, flow-ing maxi dress along with the cutest pair of Tory Burch Gemini Link T-strap sandals. Her Brazilian, wavy bundles were braided to the back in two braids, which looked super cute on her. Makeup was light but on point, and her face was pretty as ever.

"All I got to do is throw on my clothes, heffa," I said, following her upstairs to my master bedroom. I'd already taken a shower and put on body lotion, and yesterday my hairdresser had given my natural hair a silk press, so I was practically ready.

"Dang, cousin! Single looks good on you," Bree complimented me when I removed my robe and stood at my lighted mirror applying BB cream to my face.

"Don't it though? Been hitting the gym five days a week and I'm feeling good. I wasn't even trying to lose weight. Just wanted to do something to distract me from thinking about Tell all day every day, but I gotta admit that I'm loving this new body of mine," I said as I turned to take a look at my thong-clad ass in the mirror. I'd never had much of a butt, but working out consistently and doing a gang of squats daily had my little shit looking tight and sitting right.

"I might have to start going with you," she lied.

"Chile, please. You know you need to quit," I teased. Unlike myself, Breelyn was a fucking brick house. Didn't work out, ate like a 200-pound man, and her body was still on point. She contributed it to having a high metabolism or some shit, but I called it blessed. I was a size ten and didn't want to be any smaller than I currently was. Wasn't interested in being super slim or looking like a model. It had taken me a minute, but I was back to loving me just the way I was.

"You heard from David yet?"

"No, but I'm sure I will soon enough. I've been back a few weeks, so it's just a matter of time before I run into someone he's linked to. Can't hide forever, and you already know they won't waste any time telling him that they've seen me out and about. I don't want to go backward, Kota, but I'm scared that when I see him face-to-face, I'll be right back at square one," she stressed.

My cousin hated being weak for David, and I felt her pain. A whole year later and she still had feelings for him. Maybe not as strong as before but still lingering. Every night when I prayed for strength to continue resisting Montell's attempts to reconcile, I also prayed for God to break the chains David had around my cousin's heart.

"Yo, Bree, you think them niggas put a root on us or some'n?" I asked thoughtfully as I slipped into my romper. I was dead-ass serious, but Breelyn's silly ass fell out laughing at my question. "Man, I'm for real, cousin. We have never been known to tolerate shit like this from a man, but for some reason, these two lames, who just so happen to be cousins, have somehow knocked us off our square. Got us doing shit we swore we would never do. Putting up with foolishness that women of our caliber should never consider dealing with. You know they people are from somewhere in Louisiana, so I wouldn't be surprised. Punk mu'fucka done put some goddamn voodoo on me." I whispered that last part, getting upset that what I was saying was really a possibility.

Bree's ass was still rolling. "Girl, you're crazy, but I sure did need that laugh," she said, still wiping tears from her eyes before getting serious. "If that were the case, Kota, why were you able to break free like it wasn't shit but I'm stuck loving this nothing-ass nigga who means me no good? After everything he's taken me through, if I saw him today, I would probably take him back. Be living back up in that dumb-ass house with his dumb-ass baby mama and his dumb-ass son. What the hell is wrong with me?" she asked no one in particular, placing her head in her hands.

"Damn, Bree, the baby dumb too?" I asked, causing her to fall out laughing again.

"You know what I meant, silly li'l girl," she replied with a smirk. Davy was the only one in the house who had some damn sense, and she'd loved on him like he was her own.

Breelyn was a beautiful girl, and she was an amazing person inside and out. She deserved so much more than what she was getting from David, but nothing I said would be able to convince her of that. Hell, I was just now remembering my worth after dealing with Montell for all that time, so maybe I wasn't the best person to give advice anyway. It was going to take Breelyn realizing on her own that David wasn't going to change into the man she so desperately wanted him to be. He wasn't going to change because Breelyn hadn't changed. As long as she continued to let him do what he wanted and treat her any kind of way without consequence, then he would do just that. It was the same lesson I'd learned myself not too long ago.

"There go my baby." My father greeted me with that winning smile. As I made my way farther into the den, he stood from his position at the card table to hug me up tight just the way I liked.

"Hey, Pops," I said, returning a smile identical to his while I gazed up at his handsome face. This was the first man I'd ever loved, and at times it pained me to know that I let him down. He'd shown me and taught me how I was to be treated by a man. On a daily basis, he instilled in me life lessons that I should have used to protect myself from the likes of Montell Mathis, but I fell in love and disregarded it all.

As if he could read my mind, he spoke, "I love you, Dakota Layne, and I'm proud of you. Don't ever think otherwise, okay?" he said, looking me directly in my eyes. I smiled with a quick nod, blinking back tears. Pops knew me better than anyone. I was close with my mother too, but my relationship with Kasey Bibbs was sacred, honey. Definitely daddy's little girl.

"Hey, Mama," I said to my mother, who had just walked up with a beer for my father. He thanked her with a quick kiss before returning to his card game. Now, my daddy was good-looking, but Mrs. Sylvia Bibbs was Foxy Brown fine. At almost fifty years of age, Mama was still killing the game. She was a prime example of "black don't crack" with her chestnut, wrinkle-

and blemish-free skin. And best believe she stayed dressed to impress. Everyone always said that I was the perfect mixture of my parents, and for that I was glad, because these were some good-looking black folk, y'all.

"Hey, mama's baby," my mother replied with a hug. "I thought Greedy was coming with you," she said, looking around the room for my cousin.

"She's on her way back here. She got a call right when we pulled up," I informed my mother. I was hoping the call wasn't from David, because she seemed awful nervous after answering the phone, whoever it was.

The look on my mother's face said we were on the same page with our thoughts. She was the only mother Breelyn had ever known, because her mother, Layne, my mother's sister, died not long after she was born. She had my uncle Kenneth but was with us most times because her father wanted her to have a positive female influence in her life. My mother tried to be that for her, but there was always a sadness and longing in my cousin for her own mother. A substitution was great, but I thought in her eyes there was nothing like having the real thing. She loved my parents like crazy, but I thought it just made her sad that her mother was no longer among the living, and she and her father weren't close at all.

"Tell her to come find me when she gets here," my mother ordered before returning to the kitchen to finish getting the food ready. It was hard on my mother with Bree being in Florida for a year. In her eyes, Breelyn was her daughter just as much as I was, and I knew she would have been just as distraught if I had been away from her for that amount of time.

"You good?" I asked Bree when she finally made her way beside me after speaking to everyone.

"Yeah, I'm okay. I'll tell you about it when we leave," she said, not wanting to go into detail right now.

I knew the tone and the look so I didn't question her. Good thing she was staying with me tonight because I couldn't wait to get the tea. "Go say what's up to Mama. She was just in here asking about you," I told her. She simply nodded and left the room.

It was just like old times as my family kicked it and ate like it was Thanksgiving instead of a normal Sunday in the middle of summer. The women had already cleared the table and washed up the dishes. Now we sat around shooting the shit, playing cards, and drinking. Uncle Herb's wife, Janice, brought her famous peach-pie and apple-pie moonshine. This batch was super strong, so we were definitely on one tonight.

The older cousins, myself included, sneaked out back to smoke and cut up before rejoining the family. I didn't indulge in the smoking of the trees often, but when I did all it took was a few pulls on the blunt before I became hella mellow and goofy. Eyes were tight as I grinned lazily with that familiar chill feeling coursing through my body.

I was the last to come back inside through the patio, and when I emerged, I noticed my cousin Elijah, who we called Rah, enter the den with a man I hadn't seen in years. He and Rah hung together tough as teenagers, but we didn't see him much after high school because he left the state for college. He had always been handsome to me, but now, Lawd Jesus! I couldn't remember his name for shit, but when I say that he was probably the finest nigga I'd ever seen in my life, that was no lie. He even looked better than Montell, and before today I didn't think there was a man alive who could hold a candle to his fine ass.

Dude was mixed race with black and white. He sported a thick, nicely shaped beard with naturally arched eyebrows and light brown, beautifully lashed eyes. Instead of the signature low cut I remembered, he now had neat, medium-sized dreads that were pulled back and tied into a low ponytail hanging down his back. He was dressed simply in a pair of dark Levi's, a white Versace tee with red designs, and a pair of red snakeskin Nike Cortez shoes. A blinged-out Versace watch and diamond studs were the only jewelry he wore. His swag made me wonder if he had turned over a new leaf and was into the same shit as Rah. I'd never known him to be a street nigga, but it had been a minute, and people change, so you never know.

Rah, who was Breelyn's only sibling, used to be deep in the life, so he didn't come around all the time, but when he did it was a movie with us all together. Back in the day he and I were just as close as Bree and I, but that changed when he started selling drugs. He stayed away so that we would be far away from his drama. With his run in the game just now coming to a close and him having more time on his hands, his relationship with his family was getting back to how it was supposed to be. Most of his family, anyway.

Breelyn's hungry ass emerged from the kitchen, stuffing her face with not one but two slices of lemon cake. She stopped midstride when she spotted Rah. She immediately turned on her heels, disappearing to the back of the house. They hadn't fucked with each other since the night Rah beat her boyfriend David's ass after finding out he punched her in the face outside the club on some jealous bullshit. She wasn't happy about it and went off on Rah for not minding his business. Rah took that as his baby sister choosing David over him when all he was trying to do was protect her. This happened almost two years ago, and these fools still weren't speaking.

Rah introduced his friend as Giannis to family members who didn't already know him, and when our eyes met, it was like time stood still. Maybe it was the weed, but the scene was like something out of a movie. A bitch was out here stuck, only able to end the stare down when Rah wrapped me up in a tight bear hug. My cousin was talking, but it took a minute for it to register that he was addressing me.

"Kota!" Rah barked.

"Damn, my nigga, why you hollerin' and shit?" I attempted barking back, but instead, I spoke slow as hell, my Southern drawl oh so evident. I was so damn high right now, and I prayed that I did nothing to embarrass myself in front of my cousin's handsome homeboy.

"I'm talking to you and you ain't saying shit, that's why. How you been, baby girl? I been calling yo' ass all week. Fuck you got going on?" he asked, staring into my eyes with genuine concern. He, along with everyone else, was aware of my fucked-up relationship with Montell and knew that he was the reason I hadn't been coming around as much. If Rah, who hardly ever visited, noticed my absence, then it was clear how bad the shit was. Sure, I talked to him on the regular, but I skipped most family gatherings since my man wasn't welcome. Fuck that nigga now, though. I refused to put another man before my family if he wasn't my husband.

"I been good, cuz, just busy with work. I'm so happy to see you right now." I smiled up at him goofily.

"Yo' high ass," Rah called me out with a play-ful mush to my head before pulling me back in for another hug.

He knew I was a lightweight and would always give me a hard time about not being able to hang with him and the more seasoned smokers in the family. Trust me, there were a lot of them. I could drink their asses under the table, but that loud would have a bitch paranoid and wilding if I hit it one too many times.

As I caught up with my cousin, I could feel eyes on me but tried my best to ignore it. The few times I did look up I would catch Giannis staring at me intensely. He was acting like he had never seen me before or something. When he would notice me looking back, he would maintain eye contact with me for a few seconds before turning away wearing a smirk. Fuck was he smiling for? Like he knew some shit I didn't know. I wasn't on the market for a new man because I was still working on me, but it was nice to be noticed, and he was definitely nice to look at.

A few times during the conversation I tried to get a dialogue going about Breelyn being back in town so that I could see where Rah's head was at, but he shut me down at every turn. I guessed it was safe to say he wasn't trying to hear that shit. Giving up, I left to go check on my baby boo, who was still ducked off in her old bedroom.

Chapter 4

Breelyn

Reminiscing & Reunions

Kicked back on my old bed at my aunt's house, I watched television, waiting for my bigheaded brother to leave. He didn't fool with me, and I couldn't say that I blamed him, but what I wasn't about to do was sit there while he ignored me like he normally did. *Talking to everyone else in the room but behaving as if I don't exist? No, sir, I'll pass.*

I was also in here tripping off the call I received from David's mother when we pulled up to the house earlier today. How she got my number or even knew I was back was a mystery to me. To my knowledge, no one but family knew I had returned to Dallas, and they surely wouldn't rat

me out to David or his people. The same hate
and contempt they held for Montell they held for
David, even more so, and with good reason.

I played it off when I was in the car with Kota,
but hearing his mother tell me that he asked her
to call and check on me had me feeling good.
She said he didn't want to bother me but just
wanted to know that I was okay and for her to let
me know that he was thinking of me. If I needed
anything I could call her and she would get the
message to David. This was the David I missed,
and for a cool two minutes and thirty-seven seconds, I forgot all the bad and remembered the
man I fell in love with. The one who put me
before everything and everyone. The man who
catered to me and treated me like a queen.

But just as quickly I remembered all the bullshit that came along with dealing with him.
Everything about that man changed when he
ended up not being drafted into the NFL. He
became an entirely different person, but because
I loved him, I tried to stick it out. We went from
planning a wedding to me being forced into
sharing a home with him and his son's mother,
who I couldn't stand. David already had a two-
year-old son when we hooked up, and although
I didn't normally date men with children, I gave
David a chance anyway. He loved his son, and I
grew to love that about him.

But back to this living situation. One day, out of the blue, he came to me claiming that Davy and his mother didn't have anywhere to stay, and because he would never let his son be out on the streets he offered to let them stay with us until Shawna was able to get back on her feet.

I should have known off the top that there was some shit in the game, because after his NFL dreams were crushed, David hit his cousin up, got his first pack, and hit the ground running. He declined to put his communications degree to use and opted to get his money the illegal way. I didn't like it or understand it, but I stayed down for him.

I said all that to say that if David wanted to, he had more than enough money to set Shawna and his son up in a home of their own, but he chose to have them stay with us instead. I could have even gone along with Davy staying with us, but Shawna was going to have to find somewhere else to lay her head, because I wasn't having it. I didn't hesitate to voice my opinion to my man. David, in turn, informed me that if I wasn't down with it, I could move out, but there was no way I could tell him that his son's mother and his son couldn't live in a home that he paid for.

Hated when he threw his money in my face. See, I met David when I was fresh out of high school and he was in his junior year of college. I was so into this man that I bypassed college and let him be my provider. I mean he said we would be together forever so that meant he would take care of me forever, right? Wrong, and it was very naïve of me to even think that way. Every chance he got David reminded me of all he did for me and how I didn't put in on shit, so I had no say in what went on in our home. When I saw how he got down, I got a job at a nursing home in Plano off the recommendation of my Auntie Syl who used to be a dietary supervisor there. I could cook my ass off just like my aunt, so I fit right in, slangin' pots with the best of them.

Calling David's bluff regarding our living arrangement, I moved back into the room I was currently lounging in, thinking that he would eventually come to his senses and recognize how preposterous the whole *Sister Wives* situation actually was. After weeks of him not budging, I decided to do a pop up at the house to see if I could talk some sense into him. Upon entering our home, I immediately felt something was off, and my gut feeling was confirmed when I burst into my room to see David and Shawna making love. In my bed! This wasn't just a fuck for them. The way he touched her was the same way he'd touched me thousands of times. The sweet things he whispered in her ear were the same sweet nothings he would say to me that would have me writhing and panting in ecstasy as he pounded into me, much like the same way Shawna was responding to him as I stood there watching. Tears! Oh, so many tears streamed down my face. In the end, he blamed me for him sleeping with her, claiming that had I not left nothing would have happened between them. Even Shawna laughed when he said that, giving me the impression that he'd been having sex with her prior to me leaving.

Never in my life did I think David would play me like that. I was so hurt. To this very day, this very moment, that was one of the worst experiences of my life. Following that incident, guess what I did? I moved my silly tail back home thinking that would keep him from wanting to be with her, and for a whole six months, things were cool. I shouldn't have, but I really tried to make that stupid shit work. Shawna had her own space, and she took care of all of Davy's needs. I had a great relationship with David's son, but I didn't want to overstep in any way when it came to taking care of him, so I let his mother do her thing.

Like I said, for a while things were cool, but I reached my breaking point one morning as I stood in the kitchen making breakfast for my blended, dysfunctional family. Shawna and I agreed to take turns cooking, but David preferred my meals over hers, so I did most of the burning. She and Davy sat at the island eating, and I had just prepared David's plate when he walked in the kitchen to have breakfast. We ate and talked like one big, happy family. Just dumb!

When David was done, he gave his son a fist pound and proceeded to pull Shawna up from her stool at the island and kiss her. Deeply! Tongue and everything. I was so shocked and appalled that I couldn't speak or move, so I didn't resist when he walked over and did the same to me before walking out like it wasn't shit. The same tongue that was just in her mouth had just explored mine while an innocent child looked on, just as confused as I was. Shawna's ugly ass sat there and ate the remainder of her food like what had happened was normal. It didn't faze her one bit. I, on the other hand, remained paralyzed in the same spot long after she took her child and left the kitchen. I remembered thinking that maybe that shit hadn't really happened. That I was imagining it all.

It had really happened, though, and that was enough for me to wait until Shawna left to take her son to daycare and head to her job at the insurance company before I made my exit. For good. It was easy for me to leave. David never paid my moving out schemes and threats any mind. Didn't even bother calling or coming to look for me for the first week. Probably assumed I'd come home to my aunt and uncle's place, but I was long gone by the time he figured out that I'd skipped town on him. Finally, the joke was on him. He assumed I would always come back, but I was determined to prove him wrong that last time. My father had set up an emergency account for me so that whenever I reached my breaking point, I could leave and stay gone for as long as I needed. No, we weren't close, but Kenneth Waiters always looked out for me financially. I packed my little shit and bounced. Deactivated all social media and ditched my cell phone before hopping on a flight to Jacksonville, Florida. Don't even know why I chose that as my destination, but that's where I went.

One would think I would have used that time away to work on me and get over David, but I did nothing but pine over this man the entire time. Anytime I talked to Dakota the first thing I wanted to know was if David had come by looking for me again. Became giddy with excitement each time she told me how he had stopped by and how sick he looked without me. Even went as far as getting Shawna her own spot and telling my cousin to tell me I could quit playing games and come home now. For some reason, I didn't take the bait, although he'd done what I wanted him to do. The plan was to make him suffer a little longer, but deep down I knew I couldn't go back to him. I wanted to, but I just couldn't do it for some reason.

Instead of going out to meet people in Florida, I cried over David the whole year I was gone. Well, that's not exactly true. My heart suddenly fluttered at the thought of the fling I engaged in with DeMario. After dropping me off at my spot the morning after he saved me from those two perverts, when he showed back up ten minutes later, we fucked like rabbits. We didn't stop until we ran out of condoms. Then we stocked back up and went at it some more.

Sometimes it was slow and sensual and others it was fast-paced and rough. I fell in love with his lovemaking, but that hardcore sex with him was just as good if you ask me. Whichever way he gave it to me was the shit and was everything I needed at the time. Every touch, lick, and stroke was out of this world and always seemed like it was never enough. It was like I would never get my fill of him.

What was only supposed to happen once turned into him remaining in town with me for three weeks. Each time it was time for him to go, he would extend his stay for a few days. We spent that time christening every inch of my apartment as well as his hotel room, having the best sex I'd ever had in my life. Goodness! I still got chills just thinking about that man's sex game. David couldn't even hang with this man, and I was always so sure that he was the be-all and end-all of making love. Shiddd!

I missed DeMario's sex and his company, but because we'd decided not to exchange information, I would never see him again. When he actually left, I was very distraught but tried my best to conceal my true feelings. We'd agreed that our involvement wouldn't go beyond his stay in Jacksonville, and I tried not to go back on that. I tried. That man had gotten to me, and I wanted to see him again. Just a few days after he left, I broke down and searched every social media site for him. I even Googled his ass but continued to come up empty. I guessed it wasn't meant for us, but that didn't stop me from thinking about him.

"You good, boo?" Kota asked as she entered the room without knocking. That shit used to get on my nerves when we were teenagers, but she didn't give a shit then, and she clearly didn't give a damn now. Still busted up in every room like she owned it.

"I'm cool," I lied.

"Bitch, you gon' tell me who that was on the phone or nah?"

I knew she wouldn't waste any time getting the details of my phone call. When I got done breaking down the conversation between me and David's mom, Dakota looked at me skeptically.

"I'on trust that old ho. How she trying to be the middleman and wanting y'all to be together but failed to step in and say something when her son was doing you dirty? Her dusty ass knew all that time that he was beating your ass and fucking with his baby mama but wanna act like she really want you to be her daughter-in-law. I mean I know that's his mama and she supposed to have his back, but to condone that fuck shit then smile all up in your face at the same time was messy as hell. Be killing me with that 'hey, daughter-in-law' shit but really don't fuck with you. At least Montell's mama knew he wasn't shit and didn't mind letting me know it." She shook her head in disgust.

"I ain't stuttin' Millie's ass, Kota. Talking about if I need anything let her know and she'll contact Dave. Girl, bye," I spat with an eye roll. I was tired of talking about my ex. I honestly didn't want to spend another moment of my time on him. I was ready to reclaim my life and finally start living again.

I had plenty of money from the deposits my daddy and Rah made into my account regularly, so I was straight financially. They didn't want money or the fear of struggling on my own to be the reason I went back to David, so they told me if I ever decided to leave they would make sure I was good, and they'd stayed true to that promise.

Still wanted to make my own money, though, so I reached out to the manager at my old job, and she welcomed me back with open arms. My position as head cook was in no way glamorous and I didn't make a ton of money, but I liked it. Hooking up meals for the elderly residents made me feel like I was making a small difference in their lives. Some couldn't eat certain things due to their health conditions, so I made special dishes that were healthy but delicious, and they loved that about me. From the staff to the family members of residents, I always received special requests and compliments on my cooking.

My family members kept telling me that this would be the perfect time for me to go back to school, but to be honest, that's just not for me. It was bad enough struggling through high school, so what would I look like trying to take my old ass to college? I wasn't a dumb chick, but trust me when I say that ADHD is real and I didn't have the patience to be trying to go to nobody's school, online or otherwise. I'm just saying that school ain't for everybody. My dream was to one day have my own food truck or maybe even a catering company, so for now, I was content doing what I was doing. I didn't need a degree to whip pots like Mia X.

"I was trying to talk to Rah about this shit y'all going through, but you know how his funny-acting ass be doing," Kota sighed.

"Girl, I can't keep worrying about Elijah. I love him but I ain't gon' sweat him. I'm not saying that to say I don't miss him, because I do. I miss the hell out my brother. I was wrong for coming at him like that behind David's sorry ass, and all I hope is that he can one day forgive me." I shrugged.

"If yo' ass would have just apologized back, then I could have forgiven you already."

Both Kota and I looked up, surprised to see my brother's tall, lean body posted against the doorframe. His handsome face was expression-less, so I didn't know if he was serious. Was he really making it that easy for me? Nah, not Rah. That would be too much like right, but I decided to try my luck anyway. "I'm sorry for choosing

David's punk ass over you, Elijah. I love you, and I miss you so much," I said in my baby sister voice as a few tears escaped my eyes before I could stop them.

"I love and miss you too, baby girl," he said, finally smiling.

I jumped up from the bed, wrapping my arms around his waist while Kota sat her ass on my bed sniffling. *Always calling me a punk but be quick to shed some tears. Fake-ass gangster.* Of course, Rah couldn't pass up the chance to crack a few jokes at her expense, and she couldn't help but join in on the laughter.

"I'll let you two talk while I go fix us some to-go plates," Kota said, standing up from her spot at the foot of my bed, face dry like she'd never shed a tear.

"Thanks, Kota B," Rah said, calling her by the name he gave her when we were small kids. He was good for giving folk nicknames. It was kind of his thing. My cousin Tasheika, who was in the den with the rest of the family, he called Sheik Dogg. Our big-boned cousin, Chase, he called Chubb. Anytime he gave someone a name it just stuck and from that point on that was what they were known as.

"You know I got you, big cuz. Hey, you want me to fix a plate for your homeboy too? With his fine ass," she teased Rah with her tongue hanging out looking real ratchet.

"Fuck yeah, your pretty ass can fix me a plate," ol' boy countered before Rah could say anything. He was now standing directly behind Dakota with his hand snaked around her waist. The chemistry between them couldn't be missed. There was just something about the way they looked at each other.

"Aye, both of y'all need to chill with that shit," Rah said with an attitude, looking back and forth between the two.

As you can see, he hated when we talked about how fine his friends were or when one of them showed any interest in us. When we were younger, he forbade his boys from speaking to or even looking at his sister and cousin. He and all his friends were on the same shit, running the streets and sleeping around, so the last thing he wanted was for anyone he was cool with playing games or hurting one of us.

"Nigga, you ain't running shit," dude said, mean mugging Rah. "Good looking on that plate, baby girl," he said to Kota, who was looking over her shoulder at him. Her ass was stuck. As if Rah and I weren't even there, he stared at her for a moment longer before releasing her and moving back down the hallway to rejoin the others. Kota was left watching him walk away, looking real crazy because she got caught up trying to fuck with Rah. I cracked up laughing at her butt.

"Fuck you, Breelyn," she said before joining me in laughter. "That was so damn embarrassing. His ass came from out of nowhere," she hissed.

"Yeah, I came back here to show that nigga where the restroom was and heard y'all talking. That's what yo' fast ass get, Kota B," Rah joked.

When she finally left the room, my brother and I spent over an hour talking and catching up, and I didn't know how much I needed and missed him until that very moment. Rah, Greedy, and Kota B! Reunited and it felt oh, so good.

Chapter 5

Giannis "G" Williams

I Wanna Be Your Man

For the last month or so, Rah's cousin Dakota had been on my mind heavy. She had certainly grown up, and not only was baby girl gorgeous, but she was also feisty as hell. Listening to her and her family go back and forth roasting each other was the funniest shit ever. Then that look on her face when I caught her saying how fine I was was hilarious. Not to sound cocky but I'd been told all my life how good-looking I was, but I honestly never paid that shit any mind. I wanted a woman to fuck with me for me, not for how many commas I had in my checking and savings or what the hell I looked like.

I couldn't lie and say I wasn't flattered that Dakota found me attractive, though. I'd been asking Rah about her since the day we were at his people's house, but he was tripping, so getting any information from him was like pulling teeth. All he would say was that she was a writer and had just gotten out of a bad relationship not too long ago, so he wanted me to stay away from her. I understood that he didn't want anyone fucking over his family, but I had known his ass for years, so he knew I was a good dude. He also knew me well enough to know that I wasn't going to listen to shit he was saying. When I wanted something, I went after it full force, and nothing could stand in my way.

My boy didn't have shit to worry about where his kinfolk were concerned, though. I wasn't a cheater, I didn't abuse women, and when in a relationship I treated my girl like a queen. I didn't have anyone steady in my life at the moment, so I was free to spend time with and fuck whoever I chose to, but if I committed myself to a female, then that's just what that meant. It was just us. No games. I had been sticking and moving for a cool little minute now but was looking for something solid and lasting. If Miss Dakota were to give me a shot, I could fuck with her the long way. I made sure to get that number before Rah and I left that night, but she made it clear that she wasn't dating right now and would only talk to a nigga on some friendship shit. I wanted to say, "Yeah, right," but I would play her game for a little while.

Since Rah was bullshitting on the info and she only answered me a few times when I reached out, I had to find out what I could about her on my own. Dakota was very guarded, but I was bound and determined to break down her walls and make her see that giving me a chance was in her best interest. Her attempt to friend-zone a nigga just wasn't going to work for me.

I knew I wanted her for myself the moment Rah and I walked through the door and I made eye contact with her. Baby wasn't super thick like Rah's sister, but she wasn't too skinny, either. She stood at about five feet six, with nice, perky breasts, and curvy little hips that flared out and down to her small, heart-shaped ass. And her face. It was like some shit I'd never seen before. Not even gon' waste my time trying to describe it to you. All I could say was that I couldn't get her beautiful caramel face out of my head. Even those cute li'l pointy ears were cute to me. And whatever nigga was dumb enough to fuck her over would get a personal thank-you and handshake from me if I ever ran into his ass. In my opinion, Dakota Layne Bibbs was the total package.

At the moment, I was headed to the crib to continue my investigation on Kota B. Last week I'd gone on Amazon and purchased every single book she'd ever written, and I just received an e-mail alert letting me know that they'd come in today. It was so dope to me that she was an author. And not only that, but at the young age of twenty-six, she was a boss. A female entrepreneur. That shit there was too fucking cool. Now all I needed was the opportunity to spend time with her to find out everything else there was to know about her. When I Googled her, I discovered that her genre was urban fiction/urban romance. I was more into autobiographies and history, so hers weren't typically the type of books I would read, but I planned to indulge and hopefully tap into the mind and thoughts of my future wife. First up was her book titled *Shiesty: By Any Means Necessary,* by Kota B. I rolled myself a couple blunts, got comfortable on the chaise in my master bedroom, and dove right in.

Damn near five hours later, I was about 90 percent through the book, and I couldn't put it down. Even the one time I got up to go relieve my bladder, I took the book with me, holding my dick in one hand and the book in the other. I was surprised I hadn't pissed all over the commode, because I was not at all focused on what I was doing. The book was so entertaining that it had me on the edge of my seat. I'm talking murder, mayhem, sex, pain, and love. Fucking insane love. The kind you'll only find in books or on television but described by her so deeply and eloquently that it would have one thinking that experiencing some shit like that was possible in real life. This girl could tell a story like no other. One moment I would be laughing at some stupid, funny shit that one of the characters said, and next I would be gripping my dick, enthralled, as I visualized the extremely graphic sex scenes she wrote. Swore I never knew words could turn me on so damn much. Couldn't help but wonder if baby girl was fucking around like that in real life. If she was, I wanted to reenact every single scene she wrote in that book, with her as my love interest.

My original plan had been to stop by Dakota's office Friday afternoon with lunch, but here it was Monday and all I'd done all weekend was read. Type of shit was that? Even when Rah called me Saturday night telling me to meet him at Sensations, I declined. Instead of hitting up the shake joint I owned, to be entertained by some of the finest big-booty strippers Dallas had to offer, I fronted like I had other plans or some shit. In actuality I was posted up in bed, wearing nothing but my drawers, sipping Hennessy while reading one book after another. It was like I couldn't get enough. Had me thinking back to when I was dating Serenity. I would get so pissed when I wanted to be on some chill and lay up shit with her, and she would ignore my ass while reading some book. I didn't even exist to her when she had her head buried in her latest novel, and that shit used to irk the fuck out of me. I felt kind of bad because I now knew how it felt to be so engrossed that you blocked out everything and everyone around you.

After picking up food from Michelle's, I headed to Dakota's office to surprise her. I remembered her saying something about trying to eat healthy, so I got her some baked chicken with cabbage and greens. No carbs since she said she was trying to stay away from those things. I couldn't tell by the way she was smashing the cornbread, yams, and macaroni and cheese her mother made, but that was none of my business. Could have been a cheat day or something because li'l mama was most definitely going in.

"Forward me those new submissions, and I'll read them when I get home tonight. Hopefully, I can find at least three that I like, and we'll hold off on accepting any more until next month," I heard her raspy voice calling out as I walked into Dakota Bibbs Publications. Hearing her bossin' up had a nigga's dick on ten. There was something special about an independent chick about her business. Shit was sexy as fuck to me.

She had a small but cool setup here, which was decorated nicely. Expensive African sculptures and artwork graced the walls. The furniture was quality, and everything in the room blended together perfectly. The music blasting over the speakers, however, didn't exactly go along with the décor. The station they were playing on Pandora was going in, and when "Mary Jane" by Scarface went off, and the beat dropped for "Front, Back & Side to Side" by UGK, I heard them squeal excitedly before rapping along with Pimp C word for word on the verse. No lie, that shit there made a real nigga smile. If you're not from Texas, you may not understand, but if you're from the Lone Star State, you can definitely dig what I'm saying. Ol' girl, who I assumed was the one who had been rapping along with Dakota, came from the back, still going hard with her hands in the air. She jumped when she noticed me leaning against the desk and smiling. She looked awfully familiar to me, but I couldn't place her right off.

"Shit!" she hissed with her hand over her chest, but she quickly caught herself. I saw the recognition in her eyes as well, but she didn't mention knowing me. Maybe I was just tripping. "I'm sorry. I didn't realize someone was here. Welcome to Dakota Bibbs Publications. How may I help you today, sir?" she asked, turning on the professionalism like she wasn't just in the back rapping about a '64 Chevy in the yard. Shit was too funny.

"I'm here to see Dakota. The name is Giannis Williams."

"Do you have an appointment, Mr. Williams?" she asked, looking me up and down.

"I don't."

"All righty then, give me one moment," she said before picking up the phone on her desk.

Before she could dial a number, Dakota walked into the lobby area looking even better than she did the night I last saw her. Dressed down in tight-fitting Nike workout gear with her hair pulled up into a bun and no makeup, baby was stunning. "Umm, hi. What are you doing here?" she asked with her eyebrow raised.

Although she was surprised, I could tell she was happy to see me. No longer red and low from smoking weed like last time, her eyes were big, light brown, and beautiful. She was so damn pretty to me. "I'm here to spend time with you. I brought food," I said, lifting the bag of deliciousness for her to see. When she licked her lips, I smiled. Was hoping that move was for me and not at the thought of what was in the bags I carried. I knew better, though. Her ass was hungry. Heard her damn stomach growling from across the room.

"You're a trip." She lowered her head while shaking it.

"How so?" I questioned, moving closer to her.

"We don't even know each other like that for you to be stopping by my place of business with lunch, talking about you came to spend time with me." She smirked.

"Well, not too long ago you packed me up enough food to feast on for two days, so I figured I would return the favor. I can leave, though, if you feel like I'm overstepping by being here," I added, praying that she didn't ask me to leave.

"Now I didn't say all that. I'm hungry as hell, and you're here now, so you're having lunch with me whether you want to or not." She bucked at me, making me laugh. This li'l nigga here swore she was hard and it was funny to me. Turning to her employee, she said, "Mel, hold my calls and check in with Toni on that cover for Krisha's new *Liaisons* book. I want to have something dope and sexy to send her by the end of the week," she ordered before grabbing the bags from my hands and motioning for me to follow her to the back. Of course, my eyes remained on that ass the entire time. Couldn't wait to grip and smack that mu'fucka. It wasn't even that big, but it was just so round, tight, and perfect.

"Quit staring at my ass, Giannis, and tell me what made you come see me today."

"You got a nice ass, Dakota. I can't help it." I chuckled, making her laugh too. "And I already told you that I came because I wanted to spend some time with you and I wanted to feed you."

"You barely said more than a few words to me when we saw each other last month, so I'm very surprised to see you here today," she said while removing the food from the bags and setting me up to eat. She was a good woman. A woman who didn't mind catering to her man. I could tell by the way she made sure I had everything I needed before she even touched her food. I also noticed it when she packed me food to take home at her parents' house. Everything this girl did was the shit to me. The smallest gestures seemed to go a long way with me.

"I be trying to say more than a few words to you when I hit your line, but you be acting funny as fuck. And your hating-ass cousin is the only reason I didn't say too much to you at your parents' house. 'Don't make me beat yo' ass for trying to fuck my cousin.' Ol' pretty-boy-ass nigga," I told her, doing my best Rah impersonation. Must have been dead-on because she fell out laughing.

"Mannnn, say, that dude be tripping. Been that way about me and Breelyn since we were kids. He's crazy hell, but he means well." She giggled. She was too fucking cute.

"I know he does, and that's why he my nigga. I think it's just hard for him to get out of that protective mode."

Dakota nodded her understanding. These days it wasn't often that you came across loyal friends like Rah. These new niggas were on some other shit, but Rah had been raised by some real ones, and the way he moved was a reflection of his upbringing. Hands down one of the realest men I'd ever met, and that was one of many reasons he would never have to worry about me fucking over Dakota.

"The fact remains that I want to get to know you, and Rah knows that I wouldn't be on no bullshit with anyone close to him. And please don't think I didn't notice how you just skated over me calling you out about dissing me when I called you. We gon' talk about that shit," I said as I playfully mean mugged her.

"You just ain't gon' let me make it, huh?" she laughed.

"Naw, I'ma g'on and let you have that, but you gon' quit playing with me, Dakota," I said seriously. She stopped smiling and licked her lips. I could tell that she dug my assertiveness.

"So you really want to get to know me, Giannis?" She eyed me, tilting her head to the side.

It was a simple question, but it seemed to be laced with lust. It could have just been me. Couldn't figure out for the life of me why everything this girl did or said was a damn turn-on. Right down to the way my name flowed from her lips. "I do," I replied after swallowing the huge lump in my throat.

"What if I told you I wasn't ready for that right now?" she asked nervously.

"I would say that you better get ready because I'm coming for you regardless," I told her with confidence.

For a moment we sat in silence just staring into each other's eyes. While mine spoke of my determination to fight for her, in hers I could see the battle she was having between what she wanted versus her fear of taking it there with me and potentially being hurt. I understood her being apprehensive, but that wouldn't stop me from coming for her. I meant exactly what I just said, and when the time came, and she finally gave me her heart, I'd cherish and protect it with all I had. Since she didn't offer a response or any further rebuttals, I took that as a yes. I mean she didn't say yes, but she didn't say no, either.

"Now that we got that out the way, tell me about yourself. I know a little bit, but I want to know it all. The good, the bad, and the ugly," I told her before stuffing a forkful of cabbage into my mouth.

She chuckled, but the apprehension was still evident in her eyes. It was obvious that she'd been through some things, but she wouldn't have to worry about no fuck shit dealing with me. I knew that, and in due time she would too.

"I know Rah ain't told you shit, so tell me how you know whatever it is you think you know about me," she asked, finally digging into her food. She didn't bother to address what I said about coming for her, but if she thought that was the end of it, then she was sadly mistaken. She was going to be mine whether she realized it or not.

"Truth?" She nodded. "I Googled you. You're somebody out in these streets, so it wasn't too hard to get the scoop on you, Ms. Kota B," I said, relaxing back in my seat with a small smirk.

"So tell me what you found out during your research, Mr. Google."

I laughed. "I found out that you're a fucking boss. You own your own business, and you're one hell of an author." That last part made her smile, and her eyes lit up. *Damn, I would do anything to see that look on her face twenty-four hours a day, seven days a week.*

"You read?" she asked, taken by surprise.

"Not on the regular, but I ordered all of your books, and for the last few days I've been holed up in my bedroom like a fiend reading every last one. I only planned to read one, but once I got through with that one, a nigga was hooked. Was up in that bitch in my drawers, sweating like Pookie's cracked-out ass, flipping through those pages." She laughed her ass off when I said that.

"I'm glad you enjoyed them. I'm not writing as much as I would like to and I miss it," she said thoughtfully.

"Why not?"

"Been focused on helping other up-and-coming authors get their names out there, so I haven't had much time to write."

I wanted her to do whatever she needed to do to be happy. Wasn't a damn thing wrong with helping others and making your money, but I wanted her to find some time to work on her own shit. She was a damn good author, and it seemed to me that writing made her the happiest, so in my mind, that's what she should have been focused on. She didn't know me like that, so I kept my opinions to myself for now.

"That's what's up." I nodded. "So, Miss Kota B, when are you going to let me take you out? This was nice and all, but I want to take you out on a real date."

"Look, Giannis—" she started to protest, but I cut that shit off by raising my hand.

"I'on wanna hear that 'I'm not ready' shit, ma. I told you to get ready. Life is too short. Just let me get to know you and spend some time with you. I'm not asking for any more than that right now. If you say no, I'll just keep showing up here with lunch until you agree. One date, Dakota. What do you say?" Couldn't figure out why I was acting so thirsty, but all I knew was that I had to have her. Like my life low-key depended on that shit.

"Fine. One date, Giannis," she reluctantly agreed with an exaggerated eye roll. Her ass could front all she wanted, but I saw the smile in her eyes when she agreed to go out with me.

We chopped it up for a while longer as we polished off the bomb soul food. "Come walk me to my car, baby girl." I stood up and disposed of my trash along with hers before using the wet wipes I brought in to clean my hands. I opened her office door, giving her the cue to lead the way, but when she tried to move past me, I took her hand in mine and brought it to my lips for a few seconds.

The current that flowed between us in that moment caused my heart to skip a beat. Maybe a few beats. I knew for a fact that she felt it too, because she was holding her breath, looking at me as if she were seeing me clearly for the very first time. I didn't want to do too much and scare her off, so instead of attaching my lips to hers like I wanted to, I just squeezed her hand so that she would release the breath that she wasn't even aware she was holding. Man, I fought so damn hard to keep myself from tasting her lips. Her neck. Her breasts. And the treasure between her thighs. Right here outside of her office door, I wanted to taste every inch of her. Swore I had never in my life wanted anything or anyone as much as I wanted Dakota. The thought of that should have been enough to have me running for the hills, but instead, it drew me to her even more.

"This shit crazy," she mumbled more to herself than to me.

I didn't even bother responding. Didn't think she intended to say that out loud, but I knew exactly what she meant because I felt the same way. To be so caught up so fast, after only one encounter and a few rushed phone calls, was borderline insane. However, I wasn't fighting it, and I wouldn't allow her to run from her feelings or from me. I planned to take my time getting to know her and giving her a chance to get to know me, no sex involved. I wanted her to trust me 100 percent before we even thought about taking it there. It would be hard to do because of the attraction between us, but I felt like she was worth it. If we did this thing the right way, we could build something extraordinary together.

"Since you called me out earlier I promise not to blow you off the next time you call. Hit me when you ready for that date," she said when we made it to my pearl white Ford F150 Texas Edition.

"A'ight, I'ma hold you to that." I grinned before wrapping her up in a tight bear hug. Her hair and body smelled like piña colada, and I wondered if she tasted the same. I released her after placing a soft kiss to her temple. Even that bit of contact had me rising. I needed to get the hell up out of this parking lot with her before I tossed her ass in the cab of my truck and had my way with her. I needed to focus. "How late do you normally stay at the office?"

"Most days I work from home, but on the days that I do come in, I'm out of here no later than five p.m."

"Cool. I'll wait until after five this evening to hit you up then," I said, grabbing her hand again. I didn't want to go, but I didn't want to hold her up from doing her thing. Plus, I had shit that I needed to be doing concerning my own businesses. I owned several clubs and lounges throughout the metroplex, and I'd been missing in action for a few days, so it was time to get back to it. "G'on back inside so that I can get up out of here."

"Okay, I guess I'll talk to you later. Thank you for lunch." She smiled sweetly.

"It was my pleasure. I enjoyed chilling with you." As soon I released her hand I felt the loss. It took everything I had not to ask her to say, "Fuck work," and ride shotgun with me for the day.

"And I you. Bye, Giannis."

With that, she was gone, and my whipped ass sat there in my truck for damn near ten minutes, staring at the entrance to her business before finally pulling off. Dakota was doing a number on my head and heart. I only prayed that in time I would have the same effect on her.

Chapter 6

Dakota

Love Under New Management

I was literally shaking in my Nikes walking back into my building after seeing Giannis to his truck. For some reason, that man made me so damn nervous, but he also made me feel so good at the same time. Just his presence or his voice over the phone did something to me. Know my ass was usually on ten and stayed talking shit, but around him, I was chill, like I'd taken a few tokes of some bomb kush.

I was really digging him, and I had thought about him a lot since we last saw one another. When I walked up front and saw him standing there looking like he was looking, I damn near jumped up and down clapping. This man was so fucking fine that it didn't make sense. And I just loved his casual but fly style. As attracted as I was to him, I was afraid of jumping into something new so soon after ending things with Montell. It had been months, but we're talking about a damn near five-year relationship here. Completely healed and baggage free was what I wanted to be before I would be comfortable moving on.

On the cool, I was just afraid that the shit I'd been through in the past would cause problems for me in future relationships. That's why I tried telling him I wasn't ready. I didn't want to allow the hurt from the past to make its way into my situation with him. I could say all day that I wouldn't make the next man pay for the mistakes of the men in my past, but that was easier said than done. It would be tragic to have a man like Giannis in my life then lose him due to my insecurities and hang-ups. His cockiness and overall aura was everything, and I could already feel myself falling for him. His vibe was intoxicating, and I was pissy drunk off that shit.

When his hand first touched mine, I wanted to pull him back into my office so that he could spread me out on top of my desk and give me those long, deep strokes. I had a strong feeling that sex with him would be life changing. And from the feel of his mans pressing into me as he held me close in the parking lot, I knew he was working with a little something. More like a big something, but I digress. Shat! This man had already found his way inside my head, and I didn't like that. Okay, maybe I did.

As soon as I plopped down in my chair, my phone chimed, alerting me that I had received a text message. I didn't recognize the number, but I cheesed so fucking hard when I saw that it was from Giannis.

Unknown: Lock me in, baby, and enjoy the rest of your day. G

Me: Gotcha. You enjoy the rest of your day as well. TTYL!

Guessed he'd figured out that I didn't have his number stored, because every time he called, I would ask who was speaking. I deleted his contact information the night he gave me his number, hoping to get seeing him out of my head, and I also didn't want to have to resist the urge to dial his number twenty times per day. He wasn't letting me get away with that any longer, so I honored his request and saved his number again. The goofy grin I was wearing was wiped from my face when I felt someone staring at me. I looked up to see Mel's nosy ass standing in the doorway of my office like she didn't have more important shit she should be doing.

"How can I help you, ma'am?" I asked in my professional voice.

Melanie Banks and I met about six years ago when we were attending a women entrepreneurs' convention in Atlanta. We were both college students at the time. She was spending her summer working as an assistant to an up-and-coming celebrity hair stylist, while I was networking for my publishing company. We hit it off instantly, and it just so happened we were both from Dallas, so we kept in touch. She was an English major and was smart as hell.

After being on the job as a high school English teacher for less than a year, she left after being falsely accused of having an inappropriate relationship with a male student. Many of her coworkers hated on her from day one because she was young and beautiful, and in their opinion, she dressed a bit too provocatively for a teacher. They also felt she was way too friendly with her students. I thought the idea was to have a good rapport with students, but maybe I was wrong. And she surely couldn't help the way she was built. She had tried unsuccessfully for years to disguise her curvy body. Curves like the ones she possessed weren't easy to hide, and she hated that the way her clothes fit her thick body gave folks the wrong impression of her.

She was no pedophile, but at the end of the day, it was a student's word against hers. By the time it came out that the young man had made the story up and lied on his dick, her reputation had been ruined by the scandal. The few staff members she thought were cool with her began to shun her and talk shit behind her back. Because of the issues she was already having at work, it didn't take much for them to switch up and believe the worst about her. In the end, she chose not to return not only to work but to teaching altogether.

As soon as I got my company up and running, I brought her on as my assistant and editor. Hiring her was without a doubt the best decision I'd made for my business. She was precise, her work was quality, and she took pride in what she did. By working for me, she discovered that she had a knack for writing as well and she'd already put out two self-help bestsellers. Both books gave tips and encouragement to those hoping to bounce back after falling off, switching careers, and finding your passion in life. Her real passion was singing, though. Mel was a phenomenal vocalist and often sang backup for artists on her brother Juaquin's label, Triple D Records, based here in Dallas. She didn't want to be a superstar, but she loved to sing.

Now she had her nosy ass in my doorway, about to try to get up in my business. "You can help me by telling me what's up with you and that fine-ass yella boy who just left outta here," she said with a teasing smile.

"He's Rah's homeboy, and he just stopped by to say hello and bring me lunch," I said with a shrug. I wasn't one of those females who told all her business, and she knew that, but that wouldn't stop her from trying to get me to spill the beans. The only female I poured tea for was Breelyn. I trusted her with all my secrets. It wasn't that I didn't trust Mel. I guessed we just hadn't made it to that point in our relationship yet. The point where I was comfortable letting her all the way in. Females could act like they were down for you then turn around and stab you in the back. I'd been there and done that with my ex-bestie, Jada, so I was extremely cautious with my friendships after that fiasco. Just thinking about that ho had me boiling on the inside.

"So, why have I never heard of or been introduced to this friend of Rah's before now?"

"Because up until about a month ago he really didn't come around that much, Mel," I answered with a fake annoyed eye roll.

"Fine then, heffa. Keep all the gossip to yourself. You get on my nerves with your secretive ass," she said, flipping me off before going back up front. See what I mean? Nosy as fuck but she was still my dawg.

By nine o'clock that night my attitude was on ten. I'd gone to the gym, beaten traffic coming home, had dinner, and washed my ass, but I still hadn't heard from Giannis. I knew I was tripping right now, but I'd been antsy all fucking day thinking about him, and it was ticking me off that he hadn't reached out to me yet. And I damn sure wasn't about to call him. I went from rejecting calls and rushing him off the phone all month to waiting by it for him to call. Oh, how the tables had turned. I was already smitten, but the fact that he thought enough about me to stop by with lunch had me feeling him even more. Then he told me he'd read my books. That's what really did it for me. For a man to show that type of interest in me and something I loved said a lot about him. After all those years I spent with Montell, I could guarantee he'd never read any of my books. Dumb ass probably couldn't even read.

Accepting that Giannis wasn't going to call tonight, I decided to go ahead and read over a few submissions before turning in for the night. Mel had picked the ones that she felt had the most potential then sent them to me for approval. If they were good enough, within the next few days, I would contact the author personally to set up a video conference call.

Just when I got into the second submission, from a dope author out of St. Louis, my phone rang. The number was unknown, so I started not to answer, but I didn't want to take the chance of missing Giannis's call. It was possible that he was calling from a number other than the one I had stored in my phone, so I picked up.

"Hello."

"Kota, baby, please don't hang up," Montell pleaded.

Montell. I sighed and cursed under my breath, hating that I'd even answered the call. "Tell, what the fuck you want?" I asked with plenty of attitude.

"Damn, Kota, how long are you going to keep this shit up? This separation is killing me. I've apologized a million times and that still ain't good enough for your ass," he huffed.

"My nigga, sorry should be your first, middle, and last name. You're always sorry about some shit, but this time sorry just isn't enough for me. You done did me dirty all these years, and once I decide that I'm done you want to act like I'm the one who's tripping," I scoffed in amusement. He really thought that just because he apologized everything should be all good. The nerve of this nigga. After causing all this drama in my life and damaging my property multiple times, property that he couldn't afford to replace, mind you, he felt like he still deserved a place in my life. Fuck outta here.

"Kota, baby, please. I just want to come home," he begged.

"You no longer have a home with me, Montell. I've told you numerous times that I have no hard feelings, but it's over for us," I said confidently. I kind of felt bad for him. Not enough to take him back, but I still sympathized. He swore he was ready to do right, and now it was much too late.

"You was steady hollering that you accepted my apology and it ain't no hard feelings, but that's a lie, because if that were true, we'd be together, Kota. Shit, I can barely get you to pick up the phone for a nigga," he whined.

"Oh, my word! If I said we're done, then what the fuck do I need to pick up the phone for, Montell?" I shouted before taking a deep breath to calm myself. "Look, I really don't have time to go through this with you again. I'm working, and you're fucking up my flow." I knew he was about to get ignorant because he was being dismissed, so I was hanging up before he could even get started.

Just as I was disconnecting the call, I heard him call me a bitch. The next time I saw his pussy ass, it was on. Calling me out my name like he crazy or some shit. And if you were paying attention, you saw that not once did he say he loved me. I already knew what it was. All this nigga was concerned with was having some- where to live.

Not even thirty seconds later my line rang again. I picked up and calmly went in. "Montell, I'm going to run this down to you one last time, because you're obviously having a hard time getting it through your thick-ass skull. I forgive you. I don't hold any grudges against you. I could have left you a long time ago, but I didn't because I held out hope that you would change. Sadly, you never did. I've accepted the fact that you are not the man for me, and it's time that you accept it as well. Just because I forgive you does not mean we're going to be together. I can assure you that you and I will never be a couple again. Never, my nigga! There is nothing that you can say or do to make me take you back, and that's just what that is. Now if you keep hitting my jack with that disrespectful shit and name-calling, I'm gon' get Rah to come see 'bout ya ass. Now, do you understand what I'm saying, or should I repeat myself one more time for clarity?"

"Yeah, baby girl, I understand, but you got the wrong nigga," the voice on the line spoke.

"Giannis?" I cringed, eyes closed with my hand over my face, hiding like he was standing right there in front of me.

"Now you got the right one," he said. I could tell from his tone that he was smiling.

"I'm so sorry. I thought you were my ex calling back. I literally just hung up on him, and the line rang so I assumed he was calling back," I explained.

"No need to apologize. I'm just happy to know that he doesn't stand a chance of getting you back, and you ain't got to worry about sending Rah to get at that nigga. If he fuck with you again I'll take care of him myself," he told me straight up.

"You don't have to do all that. I can handle Montell." Giannis didn't seem like the average street nigga, and I didn't want him involved in some shit that had nothing to do with him.

"I ain't ask you who you could handle. I told you what I was going to do, Dakota."

"Who—" I started before getting cut off.

"I done said all I'm gon' say about it, baby. Now tell me about your day after we parted ways.

Anything interesting happen? Well, besides that fuck nigga pissing you off." He laughed easily.

I pulled back and frowned at my phone like he could see me. No, this nigga didn't check me and move on like I wasn't gon' say shit. I was about to ask him who he thought he was talking to, but I thought better of it. I would hold my tongue for now, but I was gon' have to pull his card later. Can't lie and say I didn't like his take-charge attitude. I just wasn't used to a man handling me that way. Shit kinda made my pussy thump.

"No, Giannis, nothing interesting happened. And why are you just now calling me?" I asked with an attitude.

"You missed me, Dakota?"

"No," I lied. "Just thought I would have heard from you before now." Hell yeah, I'd missed his ass, and it pissed me off that he made me wait so long to hear his voice.

"That was the plan, but I had a situation with one of my employees, and taking care of it took a little longer than I planned. And you ain't gotta lie. If you missed a nigga, let me know that. Tell me that you think about me as much as I think about you. Feed my ego a li'l bit, baby."

This man was on my line talking about me feeding his ego, and I was creaming my damn panties. The fuck? His voice was so damn sexy.

Even on the phone, he oozed confidence, and that shit there had me leaking. *Get it together, Dakota!* "Employee? What is it that you do, Giannis?" I hadn't thought to ask him his occupation before he mentioned that he had employees. Could have asked Rah, but I didn't want his blocking ass to know I cut for his homeboy.

"I'm an entrepreneur like yourself. Working for another mu'fucka ain't never been my cup of tea. I own a few clubs and a lounge, but I recently got into real estate as well. Trying to get my hands in a little bit of everything, you know?"

"I do. There's nothing like having your own. Couldn't see myself on someone else's clock, making them rich. I knew coming up that a regular nine-to-five wasn't the move for me. I'm too damn controlling. I like to be the one giving the orders not taking them. I also like to do things in my own time, so the autonomy that comes with owning my own business is perfect for me," I explained.

"Are you like that in your relationships as well?"

"Like what, G?"

"I'm G to everyone else, but to you I'm Giannis, so get that shit right, baby," he scolded me.

"Fine, Giannis, now answer the question," I said on a sigh, but I was smiling hard as hell.

"Are you controlling? Do you have issues following the lead of your man?" he asked.

That question certainly caught me off guard, and I had to think about it before I answered. I loved that he allowed me the time to get my response together. Honestly, I never really thought of the role I took on in my relationships. Selfishly, my focus was usually on the wrong someone was doing to me, and I was sure that wasn't a good thing, but I wouldn't necessarily categorize myself the way he described, either.

"In relationships, I don't think I'm controlling at all. I have no problem letting a man be the man. We're talking about a real man, though, and I surely don't have an issue submitting to or following the lead of my man, but that's only if God is the one leading him. At twenty-six years of age, I can honestly say that I've never been with the type of man who was worthy of having me follow him," I answered.

"Well, Dakota, I'm hoping I can change that. Everything you just said you didn't have a problem doing for your man is what I want you to do for me," he said in his normal self-confident, sexy tone.

Every single word that flowed from this man's mouth was a fucking turn-on. Of all the men I'd come across, why was he able to affect me in a way that none of the others ever could? It was probably that fucking voice. He put me in the mind of the rapper Lil Bibby. No, they didn't look alike at all. They both had the pretty-boy vibe going on, yet when they opened their mouths to speak, the sound that came out was so commanding, rich, and deep. Kind of expected the voice to be as soft and pretty as they appeared to be, but it was the exact opposite, with Giannis's tone carrying even more bass than Bibby's. Just imagine that. It was an unexpected sound and tone coming from such a beautiful man, but it fit him perfectly. Caught up in the moment, I wondered if my locution and the low rasp of my voice could make him as hot as his made me.

"So, you saying you want to be my man, Giannis? You want me to follow while you lead? You want me to submit to you in every way possible? You saying you want me to be your lady, baby?" I asked softly and slowly. With every question I asked, I could hear a sharp intake of breath on the other end of the phone, and by the time I made it to the last one, I heard him groan low in my ear. A satisfied smile spread across my face. *Got 'im!* When he cleared his throat, I wanted to laugh, but I held it in and waited.

"Yes, yes, yes, and fuck yes," he finally answered, causing me to fall out laughing. "Yo, you knew exactly what the fuck you was doing. You ain't slick, Kota." He chuckled. After a long pause, he said, "I'm serious, though. I want you, babe. I know that we're just getting acquainted, but I knew what was up the moment I laid eyes on you. Not the kid I knew as Kota B and not just on no physical shit, either. Don't mistake my words, because you're fine as hell, but I'm feeling your whole vibe, and I want to explore that. I want us to explore together, baby."

"Okayyy," I cooed like a schoolgirl before I realized what I was saying. I wouldn't take it back, though. Like, how could a bitch say no after he said that shit? And the way he said it. Sheesh!

"For real?" he asked like he was shocked that I'd agreed.

"Yeah, for real. Why do you sound so surprised?" I giggled.

"On the cool, I thought it was going to take a few conversations and multiple dates to convince you to see things my way," he laughed. "So, you really my lady?"

"I am. You my man, Giannis?"

"Hell yeah, I'm your man. Damn, you don't even know how happy you just made me, Dakota," he said, blowing out a shaky breath. "And we ain't just talking, trying to see where things can go. Ain't no damn testing the waters. We. Are. Together. I don't want there to be any question in your mind about what you just agreed to when you said you were my woman. Understand?"

"I do, but damn, we haven't even been on an official date, and here we are on the phone like some teenagers, talking about we go together and shit. You gotta admit this shit is insane, Giannis," I said, getting nervous about what I had just signed up for. Things were happening way too fast, and that scared the shit out of me. To have feelings this strong so early on was frightening and made me want to hang up, block his number, and avoid him for the rest of my life. A man like him could have me out there just as bad if not worse than I was when I was with Montell's ass. Giannis had dominated my thoughts and dreams for the past month, and now I was claiming him as my man. Crazy!

"Don't start doubting us already, Kota. Love don't work like that. I'm not claiming to be in love or no shit like that, but that's definitely where we're headed. You don't think I'm nervous about how fast this is moving? About the crazy-ass feelings I have for you? I am, but I won't deprive myself of you, and I hope you won't deprive yourself of me. Give us a chance, Dakota. Let me in," he urged.

"Okayyy," I cooed once again, completely sold on the idea of us together as a couple. See how easy that shit was? All this man had to do was make his request known and I was all for whatever he wanted. I was scared but not enough to walk away, so I decided to trust my gut and trust Giannis. This was going to be either the worst decision I'd ever made or the best thing to ever happen to me. I was just hoping and praying it was the latter. Lord knows I couldn't stand another heartbreak.

We stayed on the phone until a little after three a.m., chatting like some lovesick adolescents. In that time, I learned a little about his family, college years, and his businesses, and he even touched on some of his past relationships. I knew there was so much more for him to tell me, and I couldn't wait to hear all of his crazy stories.

I told him about my people, and he loved how roguish and down for one another we were. I also talked some about Montell and the changes he took me through. Didn't share too much, because it really wasn't my thing to talk about exes, but if he asked a question, I answered truthfully. I could tell he was surprised that I put up with that nonsense, but he didn't voice his opinion either way. He only said how glad he was that Montell fucked things up with me because it gave him an opportunity to show me how a woman was supposed to be treated by her man.

In a few short hours, I felt like I'd known him all my life. I'd already planned to work from home the following day, so we were going on our first date tomorrow. Giannis said he was taking me on a date every night this week because we had a lot of catching up to do since I'd been curbing him for the last month.

"Baby, I'ma let you go so you can rest up and be ready for me tomorrow."

"Okay, I'll text you when I'm up and moving around," I said.

"Sweet dreams, Dakota."

"Ditto, baby," I said before disconnecting the call.

I went to sleep with a huge smile on my face, and for the first time in a long time, I was hopeful for what lay ahead for me and my new relationship.

Chapter 7

Montell Mathis

Lost Without You

This time without Dakota has been extremely hard on a brother. I'd been blowing her up and damn near stalking her ass trying to get her to take me back, but she wasn't budging. You know the saying "You never miss a good thing until it's gone"? Well, I was experiencing that shit tenfold right now, and I was a living witness that that was one of the realest things ever said. I may sound crazy, but I never thought the day would come when my baby would decide she really wasn't fucking with me no more. She'd taken me back so many times after I'd done so many foul things that I assumed she always would.

Although I'd done my fair share of fucked-up shit, at the end of the day I really loved Dakota. Guessed I just had a messed-up way of showing it. I'd never in my life been with a female who made me feel like I was less than a man, but that's exactly what it felt like being with Dakota. It wasn't something she did purposely, but being with her made me realize all the ways I was lacking as a man. She was independent and established with her own money, but I, on the other hand, couldn't seem to hold a job for longer than a few months at a time. I wasn't built for the streets so the few times I'd tried my hand at hustling had been epic failures. In turn, I occasionally spent time behind bars and owed debts that my woman had to pay off for me. She had it, so I wasn't about to turn down the help. Sure, I wanted to be Dakota's provider and not the other way around, but for some reason, I just couldn't seem to get my shit together and do right. She didn't need me to take care of her anyway, but it fucked me up that I couldn't even if she did. Kota never threw her money in my face. All she ever wanted from me was for me to love her right, and I couldn't even do that. Now she was fed up and claiming to be done with me, but there was no way I could accept that.

Another aspect of our relationship that caused us to butt heads was our sex life. I knew Dakota wasn't satisfied with me, and that was a major blow to my ego and one of the reasons I slept around. The other women I fucked around with didn't complain about the sex. I honestly thought they were just happy to be sleeping with a good-looking man.

Some crazy shit had gone down with me when I was a kid, so sex was a touchy subject and act for me. Missionary was the only position I was comfortable fucking in, but Dakota needed more. I tried for her a few times, but for whatever reason, I couldn't have a woman on top riding me. Kota loved to ride and some more shit. Her freaky ass wanted me to have her hanging from chandeliers, serving her back shots on the dinner table, or playing in her pussy in the back of a dark movie theater. I just couldn't get with that shit. She was sexually free and needed a man who could meet her needs, but I just wasn't that nigga.

I could have easily talked to her about my issues or sought help for my problem, but as a man, I was too ashamed. I was sure she would have understood, but I just couldn't bring myself to tell her what was going on. I honestly thought that one incident was the root cause of most of my problems. When thoughts of that shit in my past became too much and I was going through it, I would attempt to take my frustrations out on Dakota with my hands.

I say "attempt" because her little ass would give me a run for my money each and every time. No lie, it was like fighting a grown-ass man. It's funny just thinking about how we used to go at it. I knew it wasn't cool for me to hit on my girl, but I couldn't help but laugh at the fact that she used to kick my ass most times. I really missed that crazy-ass girl.

As fucked up as it might have seemed, I missed the fighting the most because that at least gave me the impression that she still cared. She was no longer fighting for me, and that was a hard pill to swallow. The way she talked to a nigga on the phone was the norm for us. She had no fucking filter, and I had no idea why I continued to try her. Kota was a classy savage if there was such a thing, and she didn't care how she came at me. Still, I wanted her back.

I had to do something drastic to win her over because I was going out of my mind without Dakota. I needed her to give me one last chance to show her that I could be the man she needed me to be. She long ago stopped accepting my calls and text messages, so I was constantly calling from different numbers on those stupid apps. She hardly ever went to her office so I couldn't even catch her there if I tried. I just hoped and prayed that no other nigga had the chance to scoop her up before I got her back on team Montell.

"Ma, please! Just until I get back on my feet?" I pleaded with my mother on the phone. Was trying to convince her to allow me to crash at her place until I could afford something of my own or until Dakota let me come back home.

"No, Montell. Your ass is grown, and I'm not about to step in where Kota left off taking care of you. I did my part raising you. Did the best I could, and now it's time for you to figure shit out on your own. You'll be thirty years old before you know it, son. Time to get them priorities together," my mother stressed. Always felt like she loved Kota more than she loved me. I mean I knew I was wrong for all the shit I'd done, but I was her son, and she treated me like I was a nigga off the street.

"I know that, and that's what I'm trying to do. Esha making it hard for me, though," I complained.

"And whose fault is that, Tell? You're the one who chose to cheat and lay up with that trashy girl, so deal with it. Can't believe you did my Kota like that. Just knew she was going to be my daughter-in-law," Mama huffed.

"Me too," I said regretfully. "I'm trying to make it right, but Kota ain't trying to hear it."

"Maybe you should just focus on my grand-babies right now. Get a job, Tell, so that you can provide for your children. Let Dakota live her life. She deserves happiness after all she went through with you. I know you don't want to hear this, and I'm sorry to be the one to tell you, but Kota won't be coming around. It's time that you accepted that and move on, baby," she said with sympathy.

"I wish it were that simple, Ma. I be feeling like I can't live without her." Swore I was about to burst into tears on this phone with my mother.

"Montell, baby, I don't think you have a choice," she said before ending the call. I knew what she was saying was true, but I didn't want to believe it. I was sure that Kota still had a little love left for me in her heart, and that was all the motivation I needed to keep trying. A nigga had to keep hope alive, shit.

Mama wasn't fucking with me, so for the time being, I guessed I was stuck over here with this nagging bitch Ayesha. I hated every minute of this shit. Up until Kota put me out I had been stopped fucking with this ho sexually. Kota, however, swore up and down that I was lying and had never stopped seeing her. When I didn't come home after I got out of jail, Kota thought I came here, but I was with a whole other bitch, and I would take fucking that girl to my damn grave.

Back to Ayesha, though. I honestly couldn't stand my baby mother. Not this one, anyway. I regretted the day I met her bad-built, ratchet ass. Dakota was a baddie, but this ho here was a five at best. When you factored in her ugly attitude that brought her down to a three. Why I cheated on Kota with this boogawolf was still one of the world's greatest unsolved mysteries, and there wasn't shit I could do to change it now, short of going back in time and erasing her ass from my life. I didn't regret my baby, Montelaysia, but I damn sure regretted who I created her with.

Yes, you read that right. This ghetto bitch named my child Montelaysia. I wanted to slap the piss out of her when I heard that shit, but since I wasn't at the hospital when she was born or when it was time to sign the birth certificate, there wasn't shit I could do about it.

As soon as ol' girl popped my baby out, she started to get beside herself. When I met Ayesha, she didn't mind breaking bread, and it was nothing for her to suck my dick or fuck me on demand. Cooked big, country meals and the whole nine. Baby girl was the ultimate side chick. Could have won an award if shit like that were actually celebrated. Now that she had me in her home like she claimed she always wanted, she stayed with her hand out asking me for money. Getting her to blow me down was kin to negotiating with a fucking hostage taker. I ain't really want to fuck her, but I wouldn't have minded some head every now and then. Her house was no longer clean like it was when I used to come over to chill with her. Bitch had been fronting the whole time like she was wifey material and totally flipped the script on me.

Every dollar I'd ever given her in the past had come directly from Dakota's account. She assumed I was deep in the game, but you know what they say about mu'fuckas who be assuming. Bitch took the car, clothes, and money at face value, but in reality that was all Kota's shit.

Ayesha had no clue that it was the girl I loved and was cheating on who made it possible for me to have those things. In real life, my black ass was broke as a joke, so I ain't have shit to offer her ass. Nothing but this dick. See, my baby Kota was the type of female to hold her nigga down, and she didn't mind doing for me until I could do better. Thing was, I had no plans to do better, and I took advantage of her kindness every chance I got. My shiesty ways had finally caught up with me, and karma was fucking me over in the worst way.

I was thankful that my other baby mama, Erica, was cool with a good head on her shoulders. If I was honest with myself, when we met I was really feeling her, but I could never bring myself to leave Dakota for her. Unlike Ayesha, she had no clue that I was in a relationship when I started seeing her. When she found out, she kicked my ass to the curb with the quickness. No more pussy and no conversation unless it involved my junior. She allowed me to come by to see my son whenever I wanted, and whatever little money I was able to hustle up on the streets I gave to her for my son. Surprisingly, she accepted it without complaints. Her main concern was that my son grew up knowing who

I was. Just like she did with Dakota, Ayesha tried to make Erica's life a living hell. When she discovered that Erica wasn't checking for a nigga like that, she left her alone.

I had no clue what I was going to do, but something had to shake soon. I couldn't remain under the same roof with Ayesha for too much longer before I snapped and killed her ass. My mama wasn't fucking with me because of the way I dogged Kota, so I couldn't stay with her. My cousin David had fallen the fuck off after Breelyn left town.

Word on the street was that the nigga was playing with his nose again. Like I knew he would, he played the shit off as simple recreational use when I confronted his ass. I knew it was deeper just by his appearance. Nigga looked a mess. Like I'd done to Dakota, he had dogged Breelyn out, and now he was sick that she didn't want anything to do with him. I was fucked up without Kota, but one thing you wouldn't catch me doing was some fucking coke. The most I did was smoke weed. My black ass didn't even drink. That was due to that same bullshit from my childhood that I don't care to discuss right now. But yeah, I didn't fuck around.

I was thinking that it was time for me to take my mother's advice and reevaluate my life and make some changes. Time was running out, so I had to get my shit straightened out soon. I planned to do whatever was necessary to get Dakota back. I knew I couldn't come at her on no bullshit. Getting a job was first on my list. I felt like she would respect me more if I went about it the right way. When I stepped to her this time, I wanted to be a completely different man. I just hoped it wasn't too late.

Chapter 8

Breelyn

Brand New

Glowing. That's what folks told me I was doing these days. I had that glow, honey! Seriously, though, my life was going great, and this was the happiest I'd been in a long time. My brother and I were back tight, I had my own place and a job, and most importantly I was sucka free.

It had been a long time coming, but I had officially gotten David out of my system. Sure, I missed some of the good times he and I shared, but I didn't miss him enough to take him back. Wasn't nothing like having peace of mind. All it took was me finding out he had another baby on the way with Shawna and I was over it. I took my family's advice and stopped hiding, and I'd never felt freer. Believe it or not, I had even gone on a few dates with this dude Chino I met last month when I went to Park Avenue with Dakota. He was cool people, and although I enjoyed his company, he wasn't someone I could see myself with for the long haul. He was nice looking and fun to chill with, but we hadn't clicked. Probably never would, but it was cool to have a male friend to kick it with for the time being.

I'd just pulled into the parking garage at the galleria mall, hoping to find something to wear to a party Chino invited me to the coming Saturday. He said I was free to bring a guest, so I hit Kota up to be my plus one. I was surprised that she agreed to go, because ever since her ass hooked up with her new boo, she'd gone missing. If she wasn't working, she was spending all of her free time with Giannis. I wasn't a hater, so I was really happy for my cousin. She deserved to finally experience real love, and so did I. In fact, I was patiently waiting for my turn to come back around.

I pulled out my phone to shoot Dakota a text to see where she wanted to meet up so that we could get started on tearing this mall down.

Me: I'm here. Wya hooka?

Kota B: In front of Macy's, 2 level, heffa!

Me: Don't move. Not that far from you.

I put my phone away and began my walk over to Macy's. I was feeling myself, so I was switching hard as hell with my head held high. Must have been feeling myself a little too much, because the devil suddenly showed up and killed my entire mood.

"Breelyn?"

My name being called halted my sexy walk. *No, no, no! Not today.* I wasn't at all prepared to face David, but ready or not, he was currently making his way toward me. Tall, dark, and handsome summed up my ex perfectly. He was impeccably dressed like always, but it looked like he had dropped a bit of weight. Guessed that bland-ass food that pale bitch was overcooking for him wasn't cutting it. David was still as handsome as ever, but I was amazed by how much I didn't feel when I saw him. All this time I was scared that when I saw him, I would turn to mush, fall at his feet, and beg his forgiveness for walking out on him. I knew that my departure would be difficult for him, but I was proud that for the first time I had put my own feelings and sanity before his. For a while, I felt bad about that, but now not so much.

"Hey, David. What's good?" I said with a fake smile as I glanced around, peeping our surroundings. Wearing a pair of skin-tight, ripped white jeans, a fitted black tank, a red flannel tied around my waist, and black over-the-knee, high-heeled boots, I was glad to be looking like someone today. Couldn't have him rolling up on me when my appearance wasn't up to par. Had my own hair styled in a clean-ass blond bob, and the little bit of makeup I did wear had my face looking golden and flawless.

"Really, Bree? What's good? That's all you have to say after all this time? I mean, can a nigga at least get a hug or some'n? Act like you happy to see me, baby." He smiled with his arms extended out to me.

There was something different about him, but I couldn't pinpoint it, so I simply shrugged it off. I stepped into his embrace but kept my arms at my side. I thought maybe our bodies touching would spark something and bring to the surface feelings that I'd buried deep down, but again I felt nothing.

"That's what I'm talking about, babe," he whispered, squeezing me a little tighter.

He pulled back, and for a moment he just looked me over, and he seemed pleased with what he saw. Too bad I couldn't say the same. The smitten look on his face caused an uneasy feeling to settle within me. He'd looked at me that way so many times, and normally it caused my body to heat up and my face to blush, but today it did nothing for me. I quickly removed his arms from around me and took a step back to put some distance between us.

"You look amazing, baby. You been doing okay? Do you need anything?" he asked, being all caring and sensitive.

I guessed his ass thought I was out here down bad and destitute without him and his money. "Thank you, but I'm good. I don't need anything from you, David. I actually need to get going because Dakota is waiting for me," I said, backing up some more while looking around.

He quickly grabbed my wrist. Nothing forceful but just enough to stop me. "Hold up, Bree. Before you go, I need your new number. Moms said she called to check on you and the recording said your old number wasn't in service," he asked while rubbing his nose with his index finger and thumb, attempting to catch the drainage threatening to escape. If his butt was so sick that his nose was running like that, he needed to be inside, not spreading that mess in a crowded mall. So fucking nasty! I kept my eye on that hand, though, praying he wouldn't try to touch me with that bitch.

"I'm not giving you my number, David," I told him straight out. There was no need to fake

and shake. Had to let him know that there was
no need for us to be in communication with
one another. Had no problem speaking if I saw
him out in public, but one-on-one convos were
a thing of the past. I'd changed my number
last month, and fuck no, he couldn't have it.
Between him and his damn mama, I couldn't
get a moment's rest without my phone ringing.
I was doing just fine without him, and I wanted
to continue on this new path sans David Parrish
and his fake-ass T-lady. I knew Kota was bound
to come looking for me since I hadn't made it to
Macy's yet, so we needed to get this little reunion
over and done with. If she saw this nigga, she
was gon' nut the fuck up.

"Fuck you mean you not gon' give it to me?"
he spat as his grip on my wrist tightened.

See there? Was wondering when the crazy
and deranged David was going to emerge. Didn't
take long at all for him to show his true colors.
This nigga used to be my world, but looking at
him now I could only shake my head in disgust.
The urge to buck back overrode my common
sense as I stepped closer to him to speak my
mind.

"It means exactly what I said, David. I'm not
giving you my number. It's been a year. Get over
it, nigga, because I have. We aren't together

anymore, so I ain't feeling caking with you on the phone and shit. I take my ass to work every day, so I'm straight on ya li'l money. Even if I weren't, my people make sure I want for nothing. And you can save that shit about ya mama wanting to call me to make sure I'm doing okay, because you and I both know that Millie don't give two fucks about my well-being. If she did, she wouldn't have convinced me to stay with you each time you cheated or had your foot up my ass," I snarled before trying to snatch away from the hold he had on me.

His eyes bucked in shock at the way I was speaking to him. Hell, I was shocked too. Where this newfound confidence and foul language had come from was a mystery to me. Before I moved to Jacksonville, you couldn't pay me to raise my voice let alone talk back to David. After all this time Dakota's reckless-ass mouth was finally starting to rub off on me. Hopefully, it didn't get my ass whooped in this mall.

"Bitch, you done lost your fucking mind. Moved away and came back acting brand new like you forgot who the fuck I am. Trust, I don't mind reminding you," he said through clenched teeth, pulling me even closer.

This entire exchange was going on in the middle of a crowded mall, and not one person stopped to make sure I was okay. That's the fucked-up world we lived in though. If shit wasn't affecting a person directly, they wanted nothing to do with it. Well, unless they were recording it so they could show other mu'fuckas and laugh about it. This man had whooped my ass in front of a crowd plenty of times, and I couldn't recall one time that someone stepped up on my behalf, with the exception of Rah and Kota. They always got at him after the fact, though, and were never present when he hit me. He knew better than to fuck with me when either of them was in the building.

"She knows exactly who the fuck you are and so do I. Now take your dick beaters off my cousin before I remind you of who the fuck I am. Done already tased your ass once before, so trust and believe that I don't mind doing the shit again," Kota challenged him, causing him to release me immediately as a few giggles slipped from my lips.

Kota tasing David's ass then beating him down for disrespecting me, only to turn around and do the same to Montell when he tried to jump in to save his cousin, was the funniest shit I'd ever witnessed in my life. First time I'd seen a chick whoop a grown man's ass, too. David beat the shit out of me when we got home that night, though. Guessed the nigga had to redeem himself after getting his hat brought to him by a female. Since I wouldn't fight back, I was the perfect person for him to take his frustrations out on. But seeing him get stomped out and pissing on himself after being tased was worth that weak-ass smack down he put on me.

"Let's go, Breelyn," my cousin said, looping her arm through mine.

"That's cool. You ain't always gon' have your little attack dog with you, Breelyn. You gon' have to see me again," David threatened.

Kota stopped and immediately turned around to face him. "Attack dog? Nigga, I'll be that, but shouldn't yo' fuck ass be checking into a rehab of some sort to get a handle on that li'l issue you got, instead of low-key threatening folk? Quit fucking with that booga sugar and get your mind right," she teased, lightly tapping her nose.

Embarrassed by the words she spoke, all color drained from his face. That's what was different. David was using again. That explained why he was so jumpy, the runny nose, as well as the weight loss I noticed. How Kota knew about his problem, I had no clue, but I couldn't wait for her to give me the rundown. To see him fall off gave me no satisfaction, and it was a sad sight to see. Hopefully, he would get his shit together soon.

"And you can come for my cousin if you want to, but best believe I'll be the least of your worries. Rah gon' be at yo' head before you know what hit you," she warned before turning back around and pulling me toward the nearest escalator.

"I'm so proud of you, Breelyn. You was checking the shit out that nigga when I walked up," she said while giving me a big hug.

"I know, right? I have no idea where all that attitude came from. I just wasn't about to let that snotty-nosed-ass nigga punk me for my phone number like that," I laughed, pulling the sanitizer from my purse and applying it liberally to my hands and wrist. I had a thing about germs and always kept some sanitizer on deck.

"I know that's right. Fuck that nigga, though. Let's get our shop on," she said excitedly.

"Yes, let's get to it," I joined in. Her ass loved shopping more than I did, and that was saying a lot, because it was nothing for me to spend hours in a mall, popping tags. Just that quick I'd forgotten all about my encounter with David. I'd find out soon enough that my rejection didn't sit too well with him, and he was determined to teach me a lesson for my blatant disrespect.

***

"Dakotaaaa! I can't believe you're flaking on me like this! We planned this shit weeks ago," I whined.

"I know, Breelyn, and I'm sorry. I have several deadlines that I have to meet, and if I go all the way to Fort Worth with you, I won't ever get this shit done. Why can't we go tomorrow?"

"Because I'm working tomorrow evening, Kota," I snapped. "And we wouldn't have to go tomorrow if you didn't spend all your free time jiggling G's balls, then wanna wait until the last minute to handle your business," I called her out. Her goofy ass didn't do shit but laugh. On the cool, I felt like her ass was blowing me off to chill with her nigga. Dakota was never a procrastinator, especially when it came to her business, so waiting until the last minute talking about some deadlines sounded like pure bullshit.

"You know you ain't shit for saying that. Your mouth seems to get more out of control every day," she said after getting herself together. That much was true, so I didn't have a comeback. I'd been popping off on everyone lately, but instead of checking me, my family encouraged me to continue speaking my mind.

"And, bitch, I wish I was jiggling my nigga's balls. Do you know his ass still ain't give up the dick?" she said before sighing dramatically.

"Bitch, you lying!" I yelled, shooting up from my position on the sectional in my living room. Yeah, I was being real extra right now, but I couldn't believe what she was saying.

"I wish I was, cuzzo. Let me break it down for you right quick. Giannis and I have been kicking it for three months. I was celibate for almost four months prior to that by choice, and I went without sex for six months due to Montell being locked up. So when you calculate it, a bitch ain't been dicked down in over a fucking year!" she screamed into the phone.

"Damn, boobie, I'm sorry."

I dead ass couldn't think of anything else to say. I low-key thought she was on the other end of the phone crying. Swore I heard her sniffling. My cousin was a damn sex fiend, so for her to go this long without sex was unheard of. I was aware of her little celibacy stint, but I just assumed that by now she and Giannis were getting it in. Shit, even I'd gotten some dick in the last year, and the way DeMario put it down on me in Jacksonville I wouldn't need my pipes cleaned for at least another six months.

Whew! I missed that nigga something terrible, but I'd come to the conclusion that he'd served his purpose in my life. Being with him was the start of my evolution and me coming to the realization that David and I would never be together again. He'd changed my fucking life, and I hated that I would never even get the opportunity to thank him. Fuck it, though. Reasons and seasons, I supposed.

"Thanks, cousin. Sorry about ruining the zoo trip for you. Why don't you see if Chino's sexy ass wants to go with you? Whew, that boy dere fine as hell." She blew out a harsh breath, being dramatic.

"The fuck you calling fine, Dakota?" G barked in the background.

"Chill, babe. I was talking about Bree's boo," she tried to explain. This nigga stayed catching her saying some slick shit.

"If that nigga for her, the fuck you looking at him for?"

"Bae—"

"Got me out here thinking I'm special when you tell me that shit, but I guess you go around gassing all these niggas up, huh? Gon' make me fuck you up, talkin' 'bout he fine," he continued his rant.

"Bye, Kota. I'm gon' let you handle ya issue. That nigga crazy as hell." I snickered. G's ass was fucking loco behind my cousin, and he didn't give a damn who knew it. Hadn't even gotten the drawers yet and was already gone. When he finally got them, his ass was sure to be completely off his rocker.

Chapter 9

Dakota

Confession Session

"A'ight, boo, let me deal with my honey. Hit me when you get there and when you get back to Dallas," I said before hanging up with Breelyn.

I then turned all of my attention to my big baby, who was now lying down in my bed with his hands clasped behind his head, eyeing me with the cutest mean mug. My handsome, hot-headed, bossy-ass boyfriend. Swore fo' Gawd I'd never met a nigga like him, and I knew for a fact I was in love with his sexy ass. Had never felt safer with a man outside of my daddy and Rah. Giannis and I could talk about anything and everything, and next to Breelyn he was my best friend.

I sighed dreamily as I looked him over in appreciation. Not just for the aesthetic perfection that he was but for who he was as a person and what he had come to mean to me in the short time we'd been together. He was possessive in a good way and very protective of me and my heart. Always had my best interest in mind, and I loved it. All this and we hadn't even taken our relationship to a sexual level.

I wasn't one of those chicks with the ninety-day or six-month rules when it came to sex. I didn't have to know every little thing there was to know about a nigga before we took it there. If we vibed and I found a man attractive, I was fucking if that's what I wanted to do. I wasn't a ho or no shit like that. In fact, I was very selective when it came down to doing the do. Could count on one hand the number of lovers I'd had.

But with Giannis, things were different. Not having sex forced us to get to know one another. I'm talking likes, dislikes, passions, needs, and goals. All that good shit. This man didn't have to use sex to hold my attention. His actions and the words he spoke to me gave me life, and he was everything I didn't even know I needed. Yes, I complained to Bree over the phone a moment ago because I did become sexually frustrated at times. For me, making love was a form of communication, but that in no way meant I didn't value my relationship with Giannis because we hadn't taken it there. We were communicating just fine without it, and I believed that when the time came for us to make love, it would happen naturally and exactly when it was supposed to.

Sometimes I was glad that we hadn't gone there, because I felt if things didn't work out at least we hadn't connected our souls. Shit was intense enough as is. I hated to think negatively, but at times it was hard not to. I mean, everything was perfect between us. We argued like every other couple but it was mostly about petty shit, and we wasted no time making up. I would get in my head about it, thinking that a man like this was too good to be true and I was basically waiting for the other shoe to drop, so to speak. Like, without sex in the way I wouldn't be as disappointed if he dropped the ball and broke my heart, making it easier to get over him. I believed that was the reason Giannis was holding out on me. He probably felt like my fear was hindering us, and he wouldn't give in until he felt like I was fully invested. Finally, I got up from my lounge chair and made my way over to the bed and climbed in, snuggling up close to lay my head on his chest.

"Babe, why you always tripping like that? Got my cousin thinking yo' ass is crazy. All I said was that the man was good-looking," I said innocently. That's what my ass got, though. I knew he was on his way over and I still managed to get caught up talking shit. I was just glad he didn't hear me complaining about us not having sex.

"Naw, you called the nigga sexy and then said he was fine. Don't play with me, Dakota. Besides, I am crazy . . . about yo' ass," he said before planting a kiss on my forehead.

"You always know just what to say, honey," I said as I snuggled closer, crawling up to rest my face in his neck. He smelled so damn good. I would have to ask him to refrain from wearing this cologne. On him, that Gucci Guilty was a fucking aphrodisiac, and inhaling it was pure torture since he wasn't giving me no dick.

"I'm just speaking the truth, and honestly, I wasn't really tripping off what you was saying anyway. I was just trying to start some shit so you could get off the phone and pay your man some attention," he admitted, earning him a punch to his side from me. "Chill, Kota, before I fuck you up," he said, biting and sucking on my face playfully in return.

"I feel bad for flaking on Breelyn, but I just wanted to be with you today. When you said you took the day off, I was like fuck that zoo. I'll just have to find a way to make it up to her," I said, absently running my fingers through his thick beard. He loved for me to do that when we cuddled, just like I loved how he stroked my back while I lay on his chest. This was some shit that I could definitely get used to.

"What you tell her to get out of going this time?"

My response was laughter.

"You better not have lied on me like you did last time. Talking about I wouldn't let you out the house. You the reason folk think I'm so damn crazy, Dakota," he fussed while I continued laughing.

I was always using him as an excuse to get out of doing some shit like hanging with the girls. I would say he and I had plans or he was tripping and didn't want me to go out. I thought the shit was hilarious, but I needed to chill before he busted me out in front of my people. My honey could be petty like that sometimes.

"No, Giannis. I actually blamed it on work today."

"Either way, I'm glad to have some time alone with you," he said before kissing me twice then pulling away.

"Me too," I replied then closed my eyes, thinking of a way to say what I wanted to say to him. *Fuck it, here goes nothing.* "Baby, I need to tell you something." I felt his body tense up at my words.

"What is it?" he asked apprehensively while drawing back to look down at me.

I could only imagine what he was thinking. The last time I started a conversation this way I was telling him we were moving too fast and needed to take a break. My emotional connection to him was way beyond anything I'd ever experienced with any other man, so in my mind, my fear was justified. I was just too overwhelmed with what I felt that I needed to take a step back. As soon as the words had left my mouth, he hung up the phone on me, and at that moment I realized that I'd probably just made the biggest mistake of my life. I repeatedly called him, but he wouldn't pick up for me. I decided to go to his house to speak with him in person. Just as I snatched my front door open, he was whipping up into my driveway like a crazy person. I didn't even give him the opportunity to go off on me like I knew he was planning to. Hell, he was barely out of his truck before I was jumping into his arms, taking back everything I'd said and begging him not to leave me. The tightness and pain I felt in my chest the entire time I couldn't get him on the line far outweighed the fear I had of loving and losing him.

"I love you, Giannis. No, I'm in love with you," I finally said on a sigh, happy to have gotten that off my chest.

He lifted my chin so that he could look into my eyes, but I looked at everything in the room but him, afraid of his response. Didn't need him to say it back but wanted to let him know shit was real on my end. It wasn't until he called my name firmly that I gave him the eye contact he wanted. Although I was still a little fearful of the future and if it would always be this way between us, I had to be up-front with him about how I felt.

My admission seemed to be just what he needed to hear, because I felt his body relax as the tension dissolved. My baby licked my lips from corner to corner before covering my mouth with his pillow-soft lips. Couldn't remember him ever kissing me this deep or sensual since we'd been together. I didn't want him to stop.

When I felt those strong hands travel down to caress my ass, pulling me closer, I released a desperate moan. My body hadn't been fondled in so damn long. His touch was tantalizing. I was soon being moved and placed on my back as he hovered over me, staring into my eyes as if he could see through to my soul. Those magic hands then moved under my baby tee to squeeze and knead my breasts, and that shit felt so fucking right. I was losing my damn mind from his touch alone, and I knew that when he finally gave me the dick, I would be no mo' good.

"I'm in love with you too, Dakota Layne," he said sincerely before crashing his lips into mine.

His words had tears clouding my eyes. Over the last few months, this man had shown me more love than anyone I'd ever been with, but to hear him say the words had me floating on top of the world. And the way he was touching my body told me that today was the day I'd fantasized about since we met. His thick and long manhood was stiff, poking at the center of my tiny, lace boy shorts as he ground into me. My back was arched, and I began grinding back. I was damn near about to nut from dry humping this nigga. Hadn't done that shit since elementary school but it felt good as hell.

"You ready for me, Kota?" he asked as he brought his lips down to mine for another passionate kiss, making my body tingle all over.

Damn, I hoped he was asking what I thought he was. If that was the case, I was more than ready and told him so. "I'm so ready, Giannis,"

I moaned as he pushed my shorts to the side, dragging a finger down my slit before inserting it inside my warm place. Soon he added another. I was so fucking wet at this point. I looked up to see his eyes close and his teeth bite down on his bottom lip, which let me know he was also tripping off how drenched I was.

"Damn, Kota, that thang wet as fuck, baby. Get these shits off," he demanded, pulling at my shorts. I was more than happy to oblige. "I want you to sit on my face," he requested impatiently.

Guessed I was moving too slow, because the next thing I knew he flipped over on his back and was snatching me up, gripping my thighs to lift me, placing me directly on his face. As soon as my lower lips were introduced to his awaiting tongue, I almost jumped up off his ass. He was too quick, though, and tightened his grip, holding me in place.

"Giannisss!" I hissed as he proceeded to give me the best tongue-lashing of my life. His mouth and the things he did with that tongue of his were too much and not enough at the same time. The same passionate kisses he gave my upper lips were bestowed upon my lower ones as well. That, combined with the roughness of his facial hair tickling my bare pussy lips and that tongue flicking rapidly up and down my clit, had me reeling. We'd been at it barely five minutes, and I could already feel my nut building. I wasn't quite ready to let it go because I knew it was going to be a big one, and I didn't want to be one and done. I mean it had been a long-ass time since I'd had some action, so that shit would probably make me pass the hell out.

The hold he had on me loosened a bit. I quickly scooted down lower on him before flipping into the sixty-nine position. The growl that erupted from him let me know that he didn't appreciate me interrupting his meal.

"Gimme my pussy back, Dakota," he demanded while grabbing at my hips.

I was no longer facing him, but I could only imagine the frown that graced his handsome face. I hurriedly lowered my yoni back down to his face, while attempting to focus on what was standing at attention in front of me instead of what his mouth was doing to my body. This was very hard to do, because when I tell you baby ate the box like no other, I'm telling no lies.

Pushing his baller shorts and boxers down, I finally came face-to-face with his thick, long dick, and man, it was love at first sight. It was slightly darker than the rest of his tan body, and the thick veins gave off the strength of his tool. My mouth juiced up at the sight of it and I used that lubrication to my advantage as I took him inside, slobbering all over that bitch.

After working the shit out of the head, I pulled him out of my mouth and licked up and down his shaft like I would an ice cream cone. Taking him back into my oral cavity, I began bobbing up and down. Fast as hell at first, then slowed it down for a while only to speed it up again, going ham. He was way too large for me to go all the way down, but I was still doing my thing. He was tapping my tonsils and not once did I gag. Relaxing my throat allowed me to go a little farther down, and the curling of his toes let me know that he liked that shit. On my knees, I could really show him what this mouth do, but I didn't have that luxury right now.

As I continued to work my magic, he groaned and bucked, but he never stopped feasting on my yoni. I could really get addicted to sucking his dick. It was that damn delectable. Didn't know if I was moaning more from the pleasure he was giving me or from how much I was enjoying pleasing him. I was going so hard that when my orgasm hit, it caught me completely off guard, bringing me back to reality in the sweetest way possible. I briefly took my mouth off of him as I rode the wave of the heavenly feeling that had my entire body seizing out of control.

"Shit, G!" I cried out, still trembling.

"Fuck I tell you about that G shit?" he chastised with a firm smack to my ass.

"Okayyy, Giannis, damn!" I winced in pleasure and pain from him striking me.

"That's better," he praised, rubbing the spot he'd just hit. Just when I had recovered enough to continue, he was sitting up and trying to pull me toward him. "Now get up here so I can get up in that pussy. You can suck on my dick later, but right now I need to feel you, Kota," he explained desperately, knowing I was about to protest. I pouted and kissed the head once more before complying. "And turn around because I want to see that pretty face when I finally get inside," he instructed.

He was so damned bossy, but in this instance, I didn't mind at all. My eyes immediately went to his once I was facing him. My baby was silently asking me if I was really ready for this, and I answered him by leaning down and planting a kiss on him that left no doubt in his mind that this was what I wanted. Shit, I needed it. With my feet planted on either side of him, I lifted up then slowly descended onto him, savoring every inch of him. Nothing, and I do mean nothing, had ever felt so good.

"Ahhh, shit," he groaned low with his eyes still locked on mine.

"Mmm, shit, babe!" I yelped at the same time, both of us fighting against closing our eyes. It only took a second for me to catch that beat in my head, and when I did, I bucked off on my baby like a pro.

Last month, Giannis had handed over records of his recent physical along with negative results of every STD known to man. In turn, I'd scheduled an appointment with my physician to have the same tests run so that he would have the same confidence in me that I had in him when it came to my sexual health. Besides us both being disease free, I was on birth control, so we were good on protection. I wanted him to be able to feel me like no one else ever had.

The feeling of him inside me was amazing, and it got even better when he started fucking me from the bottom, matching my movements while hitting my spot every time. My mouth formed into a big O. It felt like I was being split in half, but it was the most pleasurable pain I'd ever experienced. After a year of abstinence, my yoni was so tight that it was akin to getting broken in all over again, but trust I toughed that shit out.

"Damn, this pussy so gotdamn good," he praised as I felt that familiar tightening in my lower abdomen.

"Giannis, I'm about to cum, babyyy!" I moaned loudly like a crazy person. Hell, I felt like a crazy person with his dick inside me. Like I was losing my mind and had been transported to another universe where nothing but pleasure existed. I was still coming back to reality when he flipped me over on my back and continued to give me that work.

We went at it for hours, and for the first time since I started fucking at eighteen years of age, I experienced those powerful orgasms I'd been craving. Spine-tingling eruptions like the ones I wrote about in my books. Puissant explosions that I was sure could only be facilitated by Giannis Williams. I was convinced that no one else could take me to the sexual heights he'd taken me to over the last few hours. I'm talking back-to-back releases with each one superseding the intensity and power of the one before. Didn't understand how it was possible for the shit to get better and better.

Never in my life had I been made love to like that. It was like he had already been introduced to my body before today. He knew exactly how and where to touch, squeeze, lick, and kiss me. A certain stroke that I needed at a particular time was delivered to my pussy precisely and masterfully, touching me deep down in my soul, connecting us for life. Nigga had tattooed his name on my shit without even knowing. Swore I was addicted and could have gone at least three more rounds had he not had to leave to handle an emergency at his gentlemen's club, Sensations. They were opening in a few hours, and he needed to take care of whatever it was before they could open the doors. He was kissing me all over my face, repeatedly telling me he loved me and would be back later tonight. I was trying to respond, but I slowly slipped into a dick coma with a cheesy, satisfied grin on my face. Heard his childish ass laughing on his way out.

It seemed that only moments later I was jarred out of my sleep by the vibrating and beeping of my cell phone. When I finally grabbed it from the nightstand, I realized I'd actually been down for over two hours. Baby had literally fucked my ass to sleep. After a good soak, I'd be ready for him to do it again when he made it back tonight.

I had texts from Giannis and Breelyn and a missed call from my mother. When my Samsung headset was turned on with my buds in my ears, I hit my mother back first. She didn't want much. Just checking on me to make sure Giannis and I would be at the house for dinner on Sunday. As we chatted, I replied to my man's text, which said he was missing me already and couldn't wait to get back to me. I told him that I missed him too and that he knocked me out with that bomb D. Of course, he thought that shit was funny. Cocky nigga knew he had some good dick, and I didn't have a problem letting my man know when he had put it down. I was so into texting him that my mother yelled at me, saying I was being rude, and she clicked on me.

While waiting for Giannis to respond to my last text, I went ahead and opened the message from Breelyn. All that she sent was an address and saying to hurry up and come get her because some crazy shit popped off and she might be in trouble. I copied the address and pasted it on the Google search bar as I rushed to my bathroom. Thankfully Google was thorough, and the address came up without me having the city. Didn't know how the fuck my cousin ended up in North Richland Hills, but I was going to get her.

I hopped in the shower and was out within five minutes. Three minutes later I dressed in some yoga shorts and a T-shirt I found thrown on my lounge chair. I pulled a lightweight hoodie over my head then slipped on my Nike Roshes and was on my way out the door.

I forwarded the text to Giannis to let him know I was going to see about Breelyn. A few minutes later as I was balling down I-635 headed west, he called my phone. I was shaking so bad that it slipped from my hand when I tried to answer, and there was no way for me to get it from under my seat while doing eighty-five miles per hour on the freeway. I would just have to hit him when I made it.

I had no clue what Breelyn could have gotten into so fast. We'd just talked earlier, and all she was doing was going to the fucking zoo. I hoped David hadn't caught her slipping somewhere. With that dope in his system he might not be thinking clearly, and because of how he was behaving at the mall, I had a feeling we were going to have to deal with him sooner rather than later.

Chapter 10

Breelyn

You Should Have Known Better

Chino and I were making our way through the Fort Worth Zoo, having a pretty decent time. I'd eaten so much candy and other bullshit that I knew my stomach would surely be aching later. Still couldn't believe Kota's punk ass had stood me up. She knew what coming here meant to me. Didn't know what it was about the zoo but we loved it, especially the Fort Worth Zoo. Her parents would bring us here all the time when we were younger, and the drive from Dallas was well worth it.

I preferred the company of my cousin, but having Chino here wasn't so bad. Just wished he would stop trying to hold my hand and hug

on me like we were a couple. We were friends
and not on that level at all. Hell, we weren't even
on no "friends with benefits" shit. Had never
even kissed on the mouth. Straight cheek action.
Lately, I'd noticed that he was on this "what are
we doing, where is this going" kick, and I really
wasn't feeling that. Although I felt like shit for
using him just to come to the zoo with me, that
wouldn't stop me from putting a pause on our
little friendship real soon. Wasn't feeling him
romantically, and I didn't want to lead him on.
That meant skipping out on the little party he
was having this coming weekend. I was kind of
pissed that I wouldn't be able to wear the bad-
ass dress and heels I'd picked out for the occasion, but I'd get over it.

Standing near the enclosure where the orang-
utans were housed, a feeling of unease suddenly
washed over me. The hairs on the back of my
neck stood up, and my heart rate began to
skyrocket. Even my palms were sweating. Never
in my life had I experienced anything like this.
Seriously thought I was having a real live panic
attack and I had no idea why. Eyes darting rapidly from left to right, I attempted to locate a
threat of danger close by that could be causing
me to feel this way, but everything surrounding me seemed cool. No one stood out as some-

one who was looking to harm me, but the physiological changes I was experiencing continued to become more pronounced.

"Bree, you straight?" Chino grabbed my shoulder, forcing me to look at him while he wore a concerned expression on his face. I was sure my pale face was flushed and clammy looking by now.

"Yeah, I'm good. Just a little sick to my stomach. I'm going to step into the restroom real quick. Don't want to barf out here in front of all these people," I nervously joked, with that uneasy feeling still sitting heavy on my chest. I looked to my left, and I could have sworn I saw a familiar face moving in my direction. I closed my eyes, inhaling then exhaling deeply before opening them again. When I did, the person was no longer there. *What was that all about?* Couldn't believe I was out here behaving like a freaking mental patient.

"Okay, let me walk you over, and we can cut out afterward. Can't have your pretty ass passing out in the middle of the zoo." He smiled, moving toward the restroom with his hand at the small of my back. All of a sudden I didn't want him touching me, but I played it off and hurried into the restroom without responding to his compliment.

I was really tripping, seeing shit that wasn't really there. Swore it looked like someone I knew. I would never forget that face. What was the likelihood, though? Here in Fort Worth, Texas, at the damn zoo for that matter? Slim to none, right?

After splashing water on my face and washing my hands, I quickly got myself together. What happened next happened so fast that I didn't have time to fully process it. One moment I was exiting the restroom, then the next I was snatched up and being led into a stall. I was scared shitless, but when I looked up into the eyes of the person who had grabbed me, my fear faded instantly.

DeMario. I smiled, looking at his beautiful face, but my bright smile soon turned into a frown. He didn't seem as geeked seeing me as I was seeing him, and that left me confused. A little embarrassed even. How could he not be happy to see me? We ended our affair on a good note, and to my knowledge, I hadn't done anything during the three weeks we spent together to warrant such an angry greeting from him. So what was his deal?

"Breelyn, what the fuck are you doing here?" he whispered through gritted teeth with his hands now clasped atop his head.

"I'm here with a friend. What the hell is your problem, DeMario?" I hissed back in a whisper. It was just now registering that I was being held in the men's restroom, and I didn't want to draw unwanted attention to us.

"A friend? Man, how long you known this nigga?" he asked with even more attitude, chest heaving up and down.

"Couple months. Why? You jealous?" I asked with a confident smirk.

"Jealous? Fuck I need to be jealous of that sick-ass nigga for? You know, you should really be more mindful of the company you keep and the niggas you get friendly with. Seems like the men you attract and surround yourself with are always on some fuck shit," he scolded.

"Really, Rio?" I was hurt that he would even say some shit like that, and it was evident in my tone. I was sloppy drunk the night we met, and he'd saved me when I was about to be assaulted. For him to bring that up was way out of line in my opinion. Like I was asking for some shit like that to happen to me. And how me being here with Chino was related to that situation was a mystery to me. I was so lost right now.

"I'm sorry, Breelyn. That shit didn't come out right." He lowered his head regretfully. "What I meant was that the nigga out there waiting for you ain't who or what you think he is."

"What does that even mean? Are you saying that I'm in some type of danger?" I hissed low.

"I'll give you the details later, but I'm not letting you leave here with him," he said real matter-of-factly.

"What?" I shrieked, tripping off the idea that he thought I was just going to go along with that. This was too much. What the fuck did have against Chino? A better question was how did he even know the man?

"Shh, baby. You just have to trust me. You know I would never let anything happen to you, right?"

I nodded as a few tears escaped my eyes. Couldn't even look him in the eyes, because honestly, I didn't know what to believe at the moment. I considered him my protector from that first night, but him being here was highly suspect and was causing me to have doubts about his intentions.

"Don't cry. I'll break it down to you when we get to my spot, I promise."

"You live here? In Texas?" I looked up, surprised.

"Later for that, ma. Just let me get you up out of here," he said while wiping away the last of my tears.

"He's waiting for me outside the door. How do you suppose I get past him?" I asked smartly.

"Shit, text the nigga and tell him you got sick, then ask him to go to the vending machine or gift shop to get you a bottle of water. He'll go one way, and we'll go the other," he told me like he had everything figured out already.

I did what he asked, and we waited, not talking to one another the entire time. Chino finally texted back, telling me he would be right back with my water. We'd passed by a vending machine on our way to the restroom, so my hope was that he remembered where it was and went back that way so that Rio and I could go in the opposite direction without running into him.

Sure enough, when we left I spotted the back of Chino's HBA Crew hoodie moving in the direction we'd just come from. Rio and I made our hasty exit hand in hand in silence. Next thing I knew we were in his car on the expressway. A million and one reasons for how we ran into one another at a zoo in Texas when I met him four months ago in a whole different state thousands of miles away ran through my head. This busted-ass Honda was in direct contrast to his bossed-up persona, and riding shotgun in this car had me looking at him sideways. That and the fact that he was saying I should be wary of a man who had been nothing but respectful and kind to me only added to my skepticism. Instead of Chino maybe I needed to be afraid of him. Minutes into the silent ride Chino was blowing up my jack.

"That's him?" Rio asked, and I nodded. "Let that shit go to voicemail for now," he said, turning back to face the road.

His jaw was clenching, and his fists were gripping the steering wheel like I'd done something to piss him off. Maybe he was hot about whatever problem he had with Chino. Hell, I didn't know. I just shook my head at the situation I found myself in. Why was every man in my life crazy as fuck?

Glancing over, I finally got a real good look at my former lover. He was even finer than he was when I met him months back, if that were at all possible. When he finally glanced my way, I rolled my eyes then turned to look out the window. After driving for another fifteen minutes, we arrived at a small one-story home where DeMario pulled around back and into a garage that was separate from the house. Parked next to us was a nice black Mercedes truck.

"Get out," DeMario demanded before exiting the car and slamming the door, causing me to jump. This side of him was new to me, and I didn't know how to take it. Had no idea what I'd done to make him so angry. As rude as he was being, I wanted to object or say something smart, but he already seemed to be pissed, so I did as I was told, not wanting to make the situation any worse.

After opening the passenger's side door to the truck, he nodded for me to get in. At this point I was annoyed. If he didn't want to talk to me, I wouldn't talk to his ass either, so the second part of our journey was made in complete silence with me refusing to even look his way. Could feel his eyes on me as I sat stone-faced with my arms folded across my chest, which clearly amused him. I could hear him quietly snickering every time he looked over at me.

A short time later we arrived at a modest two-story home in an area of Fort Worth that I'd never been to before. Hell, we might not have even been in Fort Worth anymore. I didn't know where I was right now or if I could trust the person who was claiming to be protecting me from a whole other nigga. I was tired of having so much drama in my life. For that reason, I made a mental note of the street name when we turned the corner, and now I had a house number. Removing my phone from my back pocket, I quickly sent Dakota a text. I had to get the hell out of here. Luckily I was able to hit the send button before my phone was snatched from my hands.

"The fuck you doing, Breelyn?" Rio yelled at me. "I told you not to respond to that nigga right now. Not until I figure out my next move," he added before powering off my phone and tossing it onto the couch.

"I didn't respond to him, DeMario. I was just checking to see if my cousin called me. She's going to be worried if I don't hit her up soon," I yelled back. I was relieved that he didn't check to see the last outgoing message where I was telling Kota to come pick me up. Hopefully, she would get here before this nigga did anything crazy.

"So are you gon' tell me what the hell is going on?" I asked, half annoyed and half afraid. As safe as I felt with him in Jacksonville, I wasn't so sure standing here with him, halfway across the country.

He was now at his bar on the other side of the room with a glass of dark liquor to his lips, looking at me as if he hadn't heard a word I said. His gaze on me made me feel like he could see through my clothing. Same look he had on his face when he knocked on my door that day in Jacksonville. Intense. Lustful. Like he was remembering what I looked like naked.

Umm, no. That's what I was doing. I was the one with the X-ray vision right now. Every line, plane, imperfection, and muscle on his beautiful body had been seared in a part of my memory forever. The lascivious look in his eyes made my yoni leak and caused my heart rate to double. Him treating me funny earlier was the furthest thing from my mind right now. How crazy was this shit? One minute I was thinking the nigga was plotting to kill me, then the next I was standing here inwardly praying, no, begging him to kill his pussy. *His pussy?* I sure did tell him it belonged to him every time he was inside me, so I guessed it was his. My body remembered him and craved him despite all the unanswered questions lingering between us. I was in such deep thought that I didn't notice him moving my way until it was too late.

"Heaven help me," I mumbled. It was all I could get out before I was being snatched forward by my shirt and wrapped up into DeMario's arms as he kissed like he fucking missed me.

Chapter 11

Demario "Rio" Taylor

Starving

I'd followed Chino from his home in Frisco. The original plan was for me to move on him this weekend at the so-called Players Ball he was hosting. Just wanted to keep a close eye on him until then, and I was glad that I'd made the decision to begin surveillance prior to the ball. The proceeds from the annual event he hosted were supposed to go to a certain children's shelter, but the children never saw a dime of that money or benefited from it in any way. The truth was that those babies were being abused and sold for sex while Chino and his partners pocketed the money. How someone could take advantage of a child who'd already been dealt a terrible hand in life was beyond my understanding, but Mr. Chino and his crew would get their issues real soon.

See I didn't just do what I did for the fuck of it. I was an advocate for women and children. Sex crimes against them especially pissed me off, and anyone involved in this shit was gon' have to see me.

When ol' boy pulled up in front of a nice apartment building in north Dallas, I parked far enough away from him to not be noticed, but not so far that I couldn't keep a close eye on him. I was thrown off when I saw a smiling woman walk down the stairs and get into his Camaro, looking just as beautiful as she did the night we met. *Not my Breelyn.* Was thinking maybe I was seeing shit. Couldn't figure out how the fuck she was here right now, or why I couldn't stop my body from responding the way it was to her. From day one that's the effect this girl had on me.

Back in Jacksonville, something in me was awakened the moment she entered that bar and I laid eyes on her. Unlike most of the people there who were dressed to impress, she was dressed down in jeans that were rolled up at the bottom, a fitted tee, and Chucks, so she definitely stood out. I was there on a mission, but when I saw her, I was momentarily sidetracked. That was until my targets approached her. I'd been sent by a wealthy man out of Miami to handle these two rich cats who had just beaten a rape case, and it looked to me like they hadn't learned a damned thing. Not even two months after barely getting off they were on to their next victim.

I'd watched her drink and scroll through her phone for about two hours, and shit seemed cool until the two men joined her at an elevated round table near the bar. I thought she was dead-on with her theory that she'd been slipped some type of drug, but I'd been so taken by her joyless eyes and thick body that I must have missed it. Breelyn went from buzzing to stumbling drunk within thirty minutes of them approaching her. I really couldn't wait to chop their dicks off and put a few hot ones in each of their domes as requested by the man who hired me. Thought I could kill two birds with one stone, so to speak, and that's precisely how it turned out, just not in the way I originally had in mind.

Follow me for a minute. My plan that night was to body these niggas and then fall into some new pussy before heading home to Vegas the following day, but seeing Breelyn in that condition put the second part of my plan on pause indefinitely. Pussy would have to wait until I got back home.

I allowed them to walk out of the bar with her before I made my move. What they didn't know was when I pulled her from the back seat of the Lexus I tossed a tiny tracker back there, so I had an exact location on the habitual sex offenders. Once I got her cleaned up and settled in my bed at the room, I headed back out to see about them niggas. Would you believe that I located them at another bar scoping the place out for another female? I could tell that was their game plan by the predatory looks in their eyes. They had another think coming, because by the time the night was over they would no longer be able to inflict pain on another woman.

I fucking hated rapists and men who abused women. Initially, I offered to do the job pro bono, and that was saying a lot, because a nigga like me normally didn't play about his bread. However, the man who hired me, the one whose daughter had been violated by the duo at a club last year, insisted on paying me the hundred grand to handle these niggas. He wanted to take care of it himself, but his wife convinced him to use my services instead. He had a solid alibi for the night everything went down, and there was no paper trail for the cash I was paid for the job, so he was straight, and those niggas were now dead and gone. Those rich boys had gotten away with this same shit so many times that the police had no clue who had eventually taken them out. The money and connections they had could only assist them in the courtroom. On these streets, they didn't stand a chance, especially with a nigga like me gunning for them. They had officially fucked with the wrong girl.

After sending confirmation that the job was complete, I went back to my room and watched Breelyn sleep. I didn't even know her drunk ass, but hearing her call out for some nigga as she slept pissed me off. Didn't know why that made me so angry, but it did. If I could have found out who the man was, I would've killed him that night too. Yeah, I was a little messed up in the head but whatever. Couldn't take him out anyway, because she probably cared a lot about him. His death would cause her heartache, and I didn't want that. From the beginning, I never wanted to see her hurt.

I had thought about her all day every single day since I walked out of her apartment in Florida. And here she was. In my home. In my arms, with my tongue shoved down her throat as I fisted her plump ass. Seriously, I didn't know how deep my feelings for her ran until I saw her with that fuck boy earlier. Right now, though, I was holding her as she alternated between caressing my neck and running her hand up and down the back of my head.

Never thought I would see her again, and when I spotted her with that nigga, I almost lost it. Asking me if I was jealous. Fuck yeah, I was jealous. She looked so different from when I last saw her. The sadness in her eyes was no more. Her smile was authentic. Wider. Brighter. I wondered if that nigga Chino was the cause of her newfound happiness. Could have even been that nigga David she called out for in her dreams. The thought of either possibility didn't sit too well with me. I had to let her know exactly who she was dealing with where Chino was concerned, but that would have to wait. My need to taste her and feel her insides trumped her request for answers.

The way she was currently gripping my dick with her free hand let me know that getting an explanation of why I was there today was the furthest thing from her mind anyway. It was nice to know we were on the same page. We usually were when it came to sex, though. Picking her up, I carried her up the stairs to my bedroom. The grip she had on my neck felt like she was holding on for dear life, like she was afraid I might disappear. The hold I had on her was just as desperate.

Because we'd agreed to go our separate ways after hooking up in Jacksonville, I didn't use my resources to locate her. It was an everyday struggle not to find her and tell her that I was feeling her on a level more than just some sexual shit, but I maintained. Barely. Love and relationships were bad for business. My lifestyle wasn't suited to having a wife or children, and those were the thoughts I had when this woman came to mind. She had a nigga wanting to give up this dangerous way of life and spend the rest of my days loving on her and making her happy. I had more than enough money to stop, but I was just doing my thing for the hell of it at this point. I was also very skilled at it. Not even my mother's warnings were enough to make me quit. But Breelyn, man, I swore I'd give it all up for her.

"Fuck, I missed you so much," I told her in between kisses.

"Show me how much, daddy," she moaned as I latched my mouth on to her neck. I was already on it, though. I planned to show and tell her how much I'd missed her and that splendid pussy she possessed. Breelyn's ass had me so open it was crazy.

"Can I taste her, baby?"

"Yessss, Rio, please taste her," she pleaded with that excited moan that I liked so much.

"You gotta let me go first, Breelyn. How am I supposed to take off your clothes?" I laughed lightly. She was still squeezing me tight as fuck.

"I can't," she whimpered.

"Can't what, ma?"

"Let you go. I ain't letting you go this time," she said, pulling back to look into my eyes as hers watered, touching my heart in the process.

I couldn't help but bless her with a sensual kiss after that. "Only for a second, baby, and then I promise I got you. You want me to lick my pussy, don't you?" I teased as I sucked and pulled her bottom lip into my mouth.

"I do," she whined and ground her hot pussy into me.

"Fuck," I mumbled. "Let me get you up out these clothes so I can do my thing. Please, Bree!" Now my ass was the one begging. Reluctantly, she released me but kept her eyes on me the entire time, still in disbelief, as if this moment weren't really happening. "I'm right here. I promise I'm not going nowhere. Relax for me, baby."

After briefly closing her eyes while taking a deep breath, she did as I asked, and piece by piece I slowly removed every item from her body. Still clothed myself, I took a moment to admire the beautiful frame that I'd been dreaming about for months. Her smooth caramel skin had a new glow to it, and the voluptuous curves had my dick standing at attention. No lie, baby had ass and titties for days. Slanted dark brown eyes with long lashes, a cute button nose, and heart-shaped lips all combined to form one of the loveliest faces I had ever seen. That innocent look she sported wasn't necessarily a front, but I saw past it. Yeah, she was a good girl, but she came out of her shell in the bedroom, and there I was able to see the passionate woman she really was.

I remembered her telling me that I was the only man who was able to bring out that side of her. Shit didn't really boost my ego, because I was well aware of what my dick and I were capable of, but I only wanted her to be that way with me. This girl was for me and me only. I just hoped she hadn't given my pussy away while we were apart. Another bitch hadn't even sniffed my dick since I was last with Breelyn, and that was the honest truth. I'd thrown myself into work to keep myself occupied, so sex was the last thing on my mind. Breelyn's was the only pussy I wanted anyway.

"Did I mention how much I missed you?" I smirked, finally bringing my eyes back to hers.

"You did, and I recall telling you to show me how much," she said seductively as she spread her legs wide, giving me the perfect view of her fat, waxed box.

Her hand then traveled down, and I watched for a few seconds as she made circles on her clit with her index finger before inserting it into her sweet spot. She couldn't touch my shit without my permission, and she knew that. "Move your hand. You know I don't play that," I told her, slapping it away. I cursed under my breath as I eyed the creaminess that was now on her fingers. With that, I was out of my clothes and in between her thighs, French kissing her pussy in a flash. She tasted so damn good, even better than I remembered. She arched her back and ground into me as I was literally trying to shove my face into her, feasting on her like I would never get the chance again.

"DeMario, baby, I'm 'bout to cummm," she whined and cried at the same time, body jerking and trembling out of control. That was all I needed to see to go even harder. I ran my thick tongue up and down her slit, giving her a moment to come down off that high before sending her ass right back up into the clouds. When I felt she was ready, I latched back on to that fat clit of hers and tried to suck the life out of her. Not too long after, I was drinking her second orgasm. As much as I wanted to continue devouring her, the need to feel the inside of her was more powerful.

After one final swipe of my tongue, I made my way up and kissed her lips sweetly. She took it a step further by sucking my lips and licking my face, removing the remainder of her sweet nectar. I knew then that I was sprung off her ass. I low-key knew it before, but when she did freak shit like that, I had to admit it to myself.

Eager to connect myself to her, I quickly slid inside her tight, juicy opening. The both of us were too caught up in the moment to notice that no protection separated us. We only moaned our satisfaction. All these months apart had been way too long. Too long not to feel something so tight. So juicy. So damn good. It was only after I felt my nut approaching that I realized I hadn't strapped up. Being inside her raw with the way her walls gripped me had me fighting my nut tough, and I was only a few strokes in.

"Gotdamn, Breelyn!" I groaned into her ear. Pulling out to the tip, I rammed back into her roughly, causing her to gasp. Her grip was so damn tight it was ridiculous. I was positive that no one had entered my space since I was last there, but I needed confirmation. "You been giving my pussy away, Bree?" I asked aggressively. Just thinking about the possibility had me heated. She was so delirious she couldn't answer, so once again I hit her with that deep, painful stroke. "Answer the fuckin' question before you piss me off and make me punish my pussy," I commanded.

"Nooo! I ain't gave nobody your pussy. I swear, baby, I swear," she cried out in pleasure.

Satisfied with her response, I pushed those legs so far back that her ass lifted from the bed slightly, and I rewarded her with the strokes I knew would get her where she wanted to go.

"Yes, daddy, yes! Moorreee!" she wailed in ecstasy as I pulled out again before dropping my dick back into her hard and fast, as her walls moistened even more and clenched me hella tight. Fuck the Magic Kingdom, the space between Breelyn's thighs was the most magical place on earth hands down.

"Dammit!" I groaned, biting down hard on her calf. Her shit was too fucking good, and nothing I did hurt this girl. In fact, the rougher I was with her, the wetter she got, the more she screamed, and the harder she came. She continuously begged for more and I gave her exactly what she asked for over and over again.

A short while later I had her on all fours, pounding her out, bringing us both to earth-shattering orgasms simultaneously. Falling back, I pulled her along with me, allowing her to land with her back to my chest, with my sticky dick resting against her butt cheeks.

"Guess you really did miss me," she panted, still out of breath.

"Fuck yeah, I did. You thought it was a game," I chuckled.

"I missed you too, DeMario, so much," she said low. "I felt you before I saw you today. Thought I was having a freaking panic attack, but I know it was just my body's reaction to you being so close by," she added, making me smile brighter than ever. I felt the same damn way seeing her standing there with that nigga's hand at the small of her back, staring at those ugly-ass monkeys.

Moving her to the side of me so that we could be face-to-face, we just lay there staring at one another with big, stupid grins on our faces. Swore I wasn't no smiling-ass nigga, but this girl brought that shit out of me. I was happy around her, and happy was something I hadn't been in a very long time.

I wanted to have a discussion with her about Chino before I got too deep into how I was feeling about her. Figured we could share a meal while I broke things down to her. "I'm starving, baby. You gon' cook for me?" I asked, hoping she would agree. During the weeks we spent together all we did was have sex and eat the delicious meals she prepared. I could burn too, but it was nice having someone cook for me for a change. I missed the meals almost as much as I missed her company and sex. Almost.

"You know I got you. Did you have something in mind you wanted me to make for you?" she asked, running her fingertips up and down my chest.

Her touch was making my dick hard again, but I wanted to eat before I slipped back inside of her. "That chicken stuffed with the bacon, spinach, sundried tomatoes, and cheese shit you made that one time. Been fienin' for it for months," I told her as my stomach growled just thinking about it.

"You have everything I need to make it or do we have to go to the store?"

"We may need to go pick up a few things, but that's what I want," I said, not willing to compromise. In that short time we were together, she had me spoiled, and ain't a damn thing changed.

"Okay. Let me shower, then you can run me to the store."

"Bet," I agreed before leading her to the bath-room in my master bedroom.

It dawned on me that this was the first time I'd ever had a female in my home. It felt good having her here with me, and I was going to take advantage.

After she rode my dick on the bench in my shower, we cleansed each other's bodies then got dressed to head out. Downstairs we were greeted by heavy pounding on the door and the inces-sant ringing of my doorbell followed by someone yelling Breelyn's name like a crazy person.

"The hell?" I shouted, looking to her for an explanation to find her eyes bucked in guilt. "Who the fuck is that?"

"My cousin. I'm sorry, but I ain't know what type of shit you was on because you weren't telling me anything. I texted my cousin when we first got here, telling her to come get me." She shrugged innocently.

"You thought I was gon' hurt you? Really, Breelyn? That's fucked up that you would think of me that way." I shook my head in annoyance when she didn't answer the first question right away.

I made my way to the door and snatched it open. Couldn't have her kinfolk out there acting a fool too much longer. I'd only moved here from

Vegas a few months ago, and I usually kept a low
profile. It was normally quiet around here, and I
didn't want the first time that I formally met my
neighbors to be because of some bullshit. Surely
didn't need the police showing up if these white
folk put a call in on my ass.

"Who the hell are you, and where the fuck is
my cousin?" a brown-skinned cutie shouted as
she barged up in my shit like she lived here. Li'l
mama was strapped and everything. "Breelyn!"
she yelled, pushing past me without waiting for
an answer to either of her questions. "You good,
cuz?" she asked when she spotted Bree by the
couch powering her phone back on. She rushed
to her, looking her over for injuries like I had
done something to harm her.

That shit pissed me off. I wasn't mad at her
family. I was mad that Breelyn actually thought
I might harm her in some way. Even if she only
thought it for a second, that was too long for me.
Never wanted her to be unsure of my intentions
toward her.

"I'm fine, Dakota. I'm sorry I had you come
all the way out here. Some shit went down with
Chino at the zoo, and I was tripping off that
when I sent you that text," she explained, looking at me as she spoke. I could only shake my
head at her scary ass.

"The fuck happened with Chino? Do I need to find that nigga and fuck him up?" She stepped back, looking at her cousin while waving that little .22 at her side. Her look and stance told me she had no problem following up on that if Breelyn gave the word.

"No need for that. I'm the one who's gon' handle that nigga," I interjected. Not only had I already been paid half up-front for the job, but the fact that he'd gotten as close as he had to my girl had me wanting to get at his ass even more than before. Yes, I said my girl. Fuck what you heard. I was locking her ass down this time. This shit was meant to be. Ending up living this close to her when I had no clue where she lived was reason enough for me to believe that this was fate. I'd been stuck between settling in Texas and going home to New York, and I was so glad I made the decision to come here.

"And who the fuck you supposed to be?" the Tasmanian devil addressed me.

Before I could respond, Breelyn rushed to my side to answer for me. "Dakota, this is DeMario. DeMario, this is my cousin-slash-sister-slash-best-friend Kota B," she introduced us with an affectionate smile. Could tell they were super close.

"DeMario? This the nigga you was busting yo' coochie wide open for in Jacksonville?" she asked, wearing a devious smile and looking back and forth between us.

"Kota!" Breelyn shouted before looking at me, embarrassed. Wasn't shit to be ashamed of, because that's exactly what she had been doing in Jacksonville as well as a little while ago in my bedroom.

"Quit crying, hell. Acting like I said some shit that ain't true. Were you or were you not popping that pus—"

"Kota, just hush! You so damn extra," Breelyn complained while I doubled over in laughter.

Ol' girl just shrugged while rolling her eyes. This one here was a wild one. Nothing at all like Breelyn. She was quite the character, and because she was about that gunplay, I could tell she and I were going to get along just fine.

"I'm surprised Giannis let you bring your uncouth ass all the way out here without him," Breelyn teased.

"Oh shit! I was so worried about you I forgot to call my baby back. He's gon' fucking kill me," she panicked, pulling her phone from her hoodie to call whoever this Giannis person was. Nigga must have been her man, because all that hard-core shit she was kicking when she busted up in my spot was no more. She had bumped that shit all the way down and was now on the phone explaining why she hadn't answered her phone. He was probably the only person who could calm her and make her feisty ass bow down. Couldn't wait to meet him.

Chapter 12

Giannis

Yo' Ass Gon' Learn

"I promise, yo' cousin gon' make me jack her ass up," I complained, weaving in and out of traffic on 183.

"Man, you crazy. Kota B will fuck yo' tall yella ass up," Rah laughed.

"Glad you think this shit is funny, my nigga." Not being able to reach her was pissing me off and this nigga was cracking jokes like it was all good.

"Only reason I ain't trippin' too hard is because Kota is on the way out there. I don't know what Breelyn got going on, but I'm sure Kota can handle things until we pull up. Just chill and meet me there."

"A'ight, man, but I'm still gon' get in her shit," I replied before ending the call. I'd hit him up a few minutes ago, giving him a heads-up on what was going on with his sister. Hell, I couldn't give him much information, because my woman wasn't answering her damn phone so that she could fill me in.

Dakota had texted me damn near twenty minutes ago saying some shit about her cousin being in trouble, and she was on her way to get her. All the way in fucking North Richland Hills! I called her phone as soon as I got the message, because I wanted her to swing by the club so that I could drive her out there, but her ass never answered the phone or replied to any of my texts. So by now, I was fucking heated and crazy with worry about how she just took off like that, not really knowing what the situation would be once she got there.

I got it. She was independent and used to taking care of herself, but she had me now, and I felt like it was my job to protect and look out for her. I was already crazy for her, but now that she had let me inside I was staking my damn claim for real now! She was mine, and I needed her to let me be her man all the way. Not on that trying to run her life shit, but I just needed her to trust me to be there for her in every way. Let me fight her battles and love on her was all I was asking for.

I hated that I even had to leave her place earlier, but my manager called saying he had some shit on the surveillance cameras that he needed me to see right away. Found out one of my regulars was basically using my spot to sell pussy. Had a nice little setup going, working with one of my best employees. I couldn't wait to get hold of her ass. I wasn't planning to confront them just yet. We had the cameras set up, and I wanted to make sure I had everyone involved before I moved on them. I wasn't knocking the hustle, but they couldn't hustle up in my shit. Their little scheme was fucking with my brand and my livelihood.

If I hadn't had to deal with that mess, I would have still been balls-deep in Dakota. I thought I was infatuated with her before, but now that I'd had my first taste it was a done deal. She would never be able to get rid of me. The way her body molded to mine, the way that body shivered at my touch, and the way her tight, velvety walls wrapped around my dick was enough to bring tears to my eyes. Bit my lip so hard I drew blood trying to keep myself from moaning like a bitch with each stroke. It was like every single thing about this woman was created just for me. The pussy was bomb, the best I'd ever had even, but truth be told I was already in love prior to exploring her insides. Never in my life had I met a woman like her, and I was positive that I would never find another. Her telling me she was in love with me was a shock but was just what I needed to hear. It had taken no time at all for me to fall for her, so I'd basically been waiting on her ass to catch up. When the time was right, I planned to lock her down on some forever shit. Swore I had never felt as strongly for any other female. Dakota was the one. My father once told me that a man knows the moment he meets a woman if she's someone he would marry, and I didn't believe that shit until I ran into Kota. Like my old man predicted, I just knew.

She'd already met my family, and they loved the shit out of her. My parents, my mother in particular, never really cared for the women I dated, so I never brought them around. Only time she would meet someone was when she randomly popped up at the house or something, but she never took to any of them despite their efforts to win her over.

Normally I dated women who were a bit more refined and reserved. However, those relationships never lasted long. There was always something missing, and besides great sex, I really didn't have much in common with that type of female. Only dated them because I tended to clash with that ride-or-die hood chick for some odd reason, even though they were my preference.

I loved me an around-the-way girl, but some females where I was from took my looks and occupation as meaning I wasn't down enough or that I thought I was too good. The tan skin I had from having an Italian mother and an African American father caused me to get picked on a lot as a kid. I'd been called a pretty boy and a square all my life, and folk pretty much took me as soft until they got to know me. Dudes tended to play me like that until I opened up my mouth to speak. I talked just as grimy and I fucked as many bitches as they did. Wasn't claiming to be a street nigga, but I was no punk. I didn't sell dope and I never would. I was from the hood, but I took a route different from the one taken by many of my potnas.

Rah was one of the only friends who didn't treat me differently or stop hanging with me when I didn't participate in the crazy shit they were doing in the streets at the time. That's why he was my dawg and always would be. While he ran the streets, making a name for himself, my focus stayed on school and establishing my brand. Just like a block boy, I started from the bottom. I just happened to go about things a different way. Didn't mean I wasn't with the shits. I was just low-key with it. Fucking with me, they found out real quick that I was indeed about that life and far from a punk. After having to whoop the asses of numerous niggas, folk finally fell back and let me be great. Guessed after all that time I had finally proven myself. The fact that I had to prove my blackness was some straight bullshit, but whatever.

Anyway, I had already forwarded Rah the text Dakota sent me. Since he was on the other side of town, the plan was for him to meet me there. I was already on my way to see what the fuck was going on. I needed to make sure my baby was straight. Fuck what you heard. At least she was cognizant enough to send me the text containing the address of where she was headed. She didn't play about her cousin, so I was sure she left in a rush with her mind all over the place. Her crazy-driving ass probably broke all types of traffic laws on the way out there, too. My girl was trained to fucking go, so I knew she showed up strapped and ready for whatever. That was one of the things I loved about her, and the thought had me smiling from ear to ear. I had finally snagged me a rider, and I couldn't be happier.

About fifteen minutes later, I pulled onto the block as my phone rang with Rah calling me back. "Aye, my nigga, I'm like ten minutes away. Kota hit you back yet?" he asked. I could tell he was becoming anxious about his sister's and cousin's welfare.

"Naw, man, but I just made it to the house, and I see her car parked on the street. I'm about to get out and see what's up," I told him as I pulled my gun from the glove compartment.

"A'ight, I'll be pulling up soon," he said before disconnecting the call.

Right as I was opening my car door, Dakota was calling my phone. "Kota, baby, are you okay? What's going on?" I asked while looking around the quiet neighborhood. I didn't know what I was about to walk in on, so I wanted to see if there were any witnesses out in case I had to pop a mu'fucka about my lady.

"Yes, Giannis, I'm fine, and Breelyn is okay too. I'm standing here with her now," she said, causing me to sigh in relief. Now that I knew she was straight it was time to go the fuck off.

"So why the fuck ain't you text me back or answer when I was calling your ass? You had to know I would be tripping after getting that text and not being able to reach you, Dakota. That shit ain't cool at all," I fussed.

"I know, honey, and I'm sorry. I dropped my phone in the car, and I couldn't reach it to answer you. I was speeding trying to see about my cousin. She said it was all a misunderstanding and she's here with someone she knows. Don't be mad at me, Giannis," she asked in a soft voice.

"I'm not mad, Kota. Just worried about you," I said as I walked into the open door of the house she was in.

Breelyn was standing next to a man I'd never seen before, while he sat on the arm of the sofa, looking irritated as fuck. Dakota's back was to me, but she turned when she noticed their attention shift to me. When she saw me, her face morphed into that beautiful smile I loved as she ran up and placed her arms around my neck.

"No, you didn't drive all the way out here." She grinned.

"Hell, yeah. Yo' ass gon' learn real quick that I'd go wherever or do whatever to make sure that you're safe," I said before pecking her glossy lips.

"You're so fucking sweet," she murmured before kissing me hungrily.

"Don't call me sweet just yet. I'ma fuck yo' ass up for wearing these li'l-ass shorts out the house. Fuck was you thinking?" I said, biting down on her bottom lip hard as fuck. Her freak ass didn't do shit but moan.

"I was in a rush, daddy. Just hush up and kiss me," she said before offering me her tongue.

Of course, I latched on, sucking gently. Before I knew it, we were making out like there weren't two other people in the room with us, and I didn't give a fuck. As long as she and Bree hadn't been harmed, then I was good. Was trying to get me a little sugar then head back to the house with my lady. Shit, a nigga was ready to eat then fall into that . . .

Oh, shit, Rah! I had to warn them before his loco ass showed up. Know that nigga liable to come in here busting his gun without asking a single question. Pulling my mouth from Kota's, I addressed her cousin. "Say, Breelyn, you might want to step outside and let Rah know what's up. He'll be pulling up any second, and you know he gon' act a damn fool," I informed her.

"Shit!" she and Dakota replied at the same time.

"Yo, who the fuck is Rah?" the nigga asked, jumping to his feet in front of Breelyn, preventing her from moving toward the door. Must have thought Rah was her nigga or something by the way he was grilling her with his nostrils flaring and shit.

"Calm down, babe. Rah is my brother," she said as she moved around him. Best believe that nigga was right behind her. Guessed he wanted to make sure she was telling the truth. I wanted to tell him that he should probably stay inside until they got shit cleared up, but I decided to mind my business.

"Giannis, why did you call that crazy-ass nigga? Bree really likes this dude and now Rah probably 'bout to shoot his ass," Kota fussed as she fell in line behind them.

"Shit, I ain't know what the fuck was going on. The text really ain't say shit but that she was in trouble, so why wouldn't I call Rah about his sister?" I asked, forcing her to stop to face me. Had to make sure she wasn't getting buck with a nigga.

"I didn't mean it like that, baby. Just come on so we can stop him before he sets it off in front of this man house," she said with a kiss before pulling me along.

When we made it outside, Rah already had his gun pointed at dude. Breelyn was in the middle of the two, hands up, trying to keep the peace. What really surprised me was the fact that ol' boy had a gun pointed right back at Rah, which caused me to pull my Glock .27 out on him. I ain't had shit against dude, and I could tell he was someone important to Breelyn by the look in her eyes, but Rah was my boy, so I wouldn't hesitate to lay his ass down if he jumped stupid.

"Y'all, put the damn guns down!" Dakota pleaded, her words falling on deaf ears. "Giannis, please get him!" she yelled, turning to me for help when neither man complied. Her eyes bucked and she smirked when she noticed the gun in my hand.

"Sorry, baby. No can do." I shrugged with my eyes still on the nigga with the gun pointed at my best friend.

"Elijah!" she yelled when she saw I wasn't going to be any help. Hated to see my baby so worked up but I wasn't putting a gotdamn thing down until ol' boy did.

"Rio, please! He's my brother," Breelyn begged, turning to face him.

He kept his eyes on Rah, but her palm against his face calmed the storm raging in his eyes. After what seemed like a few minutes but was actually much shorter, he backed down. "You got it, baby." He simpered in Rah's direction as he lowered his weapon. Dude had an unsettling look in his eyes. Like he was just as crazy if not crazier than Rah, and that was saying something.

When Rah finally lowered his gun, I followed suit as he pulled Breelyn beside him.

"Now y'all want to tell me what the fuck going on?" he asked with his eyes locked on dude.

"Talk to your sister, nigga. I answer to no one. And just know that's the last mu'fuckin' time you gon' pull a gun on me. Next time you better shoot or else," he challenged.

"Fuck you gon' do, nigga? Tal'm 'bout or else! For this one here or that one there," he said, nodding at Bree and Kota, "I'll kill yo' mufuckin ass. Straight up," Rah countered.

"Yeah, whatever," was all dude said before heading inside.

He was bold as fuck turning his back on a man who just had a gun pointed at him. Even Rah stood there wide-eyed. Luckily for that nigga Rio, Rah wasn't the type of fuck boy who would shoot you in the back. His crazy ass wanted to look you right in the eye before he took you off the set.

"Rio, wait." Bree started to go after him but was stopped by her brother.

"Naw, fuck that nigga. What you need to be doing is explaining to us why the fuck you had us drive all the way out here talking about you was in trouble, and now you trying to save this nigga. Type of shit is that?"

"Look, I met Rio in Jacksonville. He helped me out of a situation where some dudes were about to attack me when I was drunk. He basically saved my life, Elijah. After he left Jacksonville, I didn't talk to him again, but he ran up on me while I was at the zoo with Chino. He forced me to leave with him because of some beef or something he got going on with dude. I haven't had a chance to get the full story from him, but I trust that he had a reason for doing what he did. I was just a little shook at first, because I hadn't seen him in months and he just popped up out of the blue and snatched me. Talking about he had to get me away from Chino," she explained as Rah continued to look at her skeptically.

My question was, what the fuck did he know about Chino? Even I was a little leery of him when Breelyn had first introduced him to us. I had gone so far as to bring it up to Kota, but she said he was cool. I didn't push, but I damn sure kept my eyes on him when he was around.

"Say, y'all either get the fuck off my lawn or come inside so I can explain what's going on," dude barked before walking back inside. On his way, he was mumbling some shit about how hungry he was, and we were getting in the way of him getting his stuffed chicken. Yeah, this mu'fucka was crazy as hell.

"Rah, let's just go hear this nigga out so I can get my girl home," I said, looking to my longtime friend, who nodded in agreement.

"Daddy, that was so sexy how you pulled that gun out. You know I like that gangsta shit," Kota whispered, causing me to laugh out loud.

"I ain't no gangsta, baby girl, but I couldn't let dude pull out on my boy like that. But you can still show me how sexy you thought that shit was when we get home. You spending the night at my place, right?" I asked as we walked back inside the house with me pressed into her backside, arms wrapped around her waist. My third leg was aching to finish what we started earlier, and I was sure she could feel him.

"Cut that bullshit out so we can see what's up with this fool," Rah snapped aggressively.

I turned to him to find him glaring at us with his face all screwed up. "Shut yo' ol' hating, angry ass up, nigga. I'on know how many times I got to tell you that you ain't running shit over this way," I told him before turning back to Kota for my answer. He still hated the fact that I was in a relationship with his cousin, although on one occasion he told me he would rather see her with me than anyone else. Nigga turned his nose up at us every chance he got, but I felt like in his own way he had given us his blessing, and that was good enough for me.

"Yeah, babe, we can go to your place tonight," Kota cooed before tilting her head back to kiss my lips.

"Follow me," Rio had said, interrupting our moment. He began leading us to a room in the back of his home.

He had to enter some type of code to gain access to the room, which threw me off a little. Once inside, he flipped on the light switch. All of our eyes traveled around, trying to figure out what the hell he had going on. The walls in the room were painted a dark gray, damn near black, giving the room a gloomy feel. It was nothing like what you saw walking into his home. His shit was dope as hell with warm colors and a contemporary design throughout. I only knew shit like that because I'd been hands-on in designing every one of my spots. One step in this room and my first thought was that the nigga was five-o.

Pictures that looked more like mug shots of different individuals were plastered all over a huge board on one wall, with high-tech monitors and computers mounted on another. I had to do a double take when I noticed pictures of that fool Chino. The one that stood out the most was of him fastening his pants as he stood over a chick who lay naked on a concrete floor. Thing was, the girl looked young as fuck. Like barely in her teens young.

"What the fuck?" Breelyn shouted once her eyes landed on the picture. Her eyes kept going between that picture and another of two geeky-looking niggas talking to a female in a bar. Her eyes then rested on Rio in confusion, but he avoided her gaze as he spoke.

"I ain't about to go all into too much detail about what it is that I do, but I'm telling you what I'm about to tell you for Breelyn's peace of mind only. I was paid to handle this nigga Pacino Clark," he said, pointing to the picture we all were now focused on. "Who sent me is not really important. All that matters is that by tomorrow night that nigga gon' be dealt with. The reason is because he fucked some really high-up folk out of a whole lot of money and they want him to pay. After following the nigga, I found out some other shit he had going on, giving me even more of a reason to take care of him. He's been a part of a human-trafficking ring for some time now, and as you can see, his perverted ass likes to test the product. The girl in the picture was abducted from a bus stop a year ago. She was only about thirteen at the time this picture was taken. I was able to get her out, but she's pretty fucked up from all the shit these people took her through."

"Yo, you twelve, nigga?" Rah asked the question that was floating through my head.

"Fuck naw. I ain't no pig, muthafucka," he responded, taking offense, but he didn't offer more information about who he worked for or what he meant by saying that Chino would be dealt with by tomorrow. I mean I got it, and I was sure Rah did too, but I wasn't sure if the girls caught on. After hearing the shit that the nigga was into, I wanted to kill his ass myself. I didn't know where Rio came from, but I was glad he was able to get Breelyn away from him before anything bad happened to her. By the looks they shot each other, I could tell that Dakota and Rah felt the same way. Breelyn, on the other hand, just looked shocked by what she was hearing. Clearly, she didn't know what type of niggas she was dealing with where Rio or Chino were concerned.

"I told you that nigga wasn't right." I nudged Kota.

"You sure did, but I didn't pick up on it. That nigga sick as fuck. Little girls? That shit crazy," Dakota replied, shaking her head in disbelief.

"Well, you do what you gotta do, and I appreciate you looking out for my sister in Jacksonville as well as today, but we 'bout to roll. Let's go,

Greedy," Rah demanded while attempting to usher his sister from the room.

"I'm staying here, Elijah." She yanked away in protest.

"No, the fuck you ain't," he said, mugging her.

"It's cool, cousin. She can drive my car back to Dallas, and I'll ride with Giannis," Dakota offered.

"You two niggas hard of hearing or nah?" he spat, looking like he was ready to put hands on both of them.

"Aye, chill with the way you talking to my lady, nigga." I stepped up, earning me an ugly frown from him, like that shit was supposed to move me. I mugged his angry ass right back. Best friend or not, he wasn't gon' be talking to Dakota like that. I knew he was mad, but fuck what you heard. He needed to watch how he handled mine.

"Like I said, she ain't staying. I'on know this nigga like that to be leaving my sister out here with him," Rah said, waving off my words.

"You gon' quit talking like I ain't standing here, nigga. I don't give a fuck if you know me or not. She does, and she knows I wouldn't let anything happen to her," he said, pointing to Breelyn. "Besides, I'm hungry as fuck and she still ain't cooked my fucking food," he said, now eyeing Breelyn, who blushed while playfully rolling her eyes.

"Greedy, bring ya ass on," Rah said with finality as he made his way out of the room with Dakota and me close behind.

I was over all this shit and was just trying to get back to Dallas. It was clear that Breelyn wasn't going anywhere. She asked ol' boy to give her a minute to calm her brother down and they could leave afterward. Outside, Kota gave Breelyn her keys then hopped in the passenger side of my truck. Breelyn and Rah were still arguing when we pulled off. My girl was safe, and now it was time for her to make me feel good after making me worry about her ass.

Seemed like she read my mind, because she quickly pulled my dick out and deep throated me right as I hopped on the expressway headed back to Dallas. I could already tell that tonight was going to be quite interesting.

Chapter 13

Elijah "Rah" Waiters

I Ain't Wrapped Too Tight

"Yo, Breelyn, you trying the fuck out of me right now," I stressed as my sister stood there trying to convince me to let her stay out here with a man I knew nothing about. Sure, she was grown and could do what she wanted, but I wasn't trying to have another nigga like David on my hands. Until I felt like this nigga was a grand, I wasn't feeling my sister being around him. He was disrespectful as fuck, which didn't help the situation at all. Nigga had the nerve to pull his gun on me. And I didn't give a damn about me pulling out on him first. Fuck y'all. I hated to admit the nigga had heart, though, and didn't even blink when I drew down on him. Still, I could take no chances with my sister.

In addition to the current issue with Greedy, I was having a hard time accepting the fact that Giannis's bitch ass was fucking my cousin. Kota was more like a sister to me, and I knew her well, so off the rip, I knew trying to keep them apart would be useless. With the way they were making googly eyes at each other that night at my aunt's place, I should have known his ol' light, bright ass would go after her. Now this shit with my sister was about to add to my stress. Like I didn't already have enough going on in my life.

"I'm not though, Elijah. I promise you, DeMario ain't on no bullshit. This won't be a repeat of the David situation. I know that's what you're thinking," she pouted with her arms folded across her chest.

"You're damn right that's what I'm thinking. I'm not trying to see you go through that shit again, Greedy. And apparently you thought he was on some fuck shit, based on that SOS text you sent Kota," I said, calling her out. She couldn't do shit but roll her eyes.

That nigga David broke my baby all the way down, stripping her of her self-confidence while damaging our relationship in the process. That would never happen again if I had a say in it. I would never take things so far as not speaking to my own sister for that length of time again, though. As the oldest, I knew that was childish and petty on my part, but I was hurt beyond words when she turned on me for the nigga who was going upside her head. Because of my pride, I lived without half of my heart for two fucking years. Kota kept me up to date on what was going on with her, and I kept money in her account so that she could stay away as long as she needed to. I was just glad she finally came to her senses and left the nigga alone.

"Just trust me this one last time, brother," she begged me, looking like a sad puppy. She knew I couldn't take it when she did that. As hardcore as I was, I was a sucker when it came to her and Kota with these sad faces.

"A'ight, man. Yo' slick ass better call me or text me every so often so I'll know you're straight and when you're on your way back home," I instructed. "Don't make me have to fuck that nigga up, Breelyn," I added to let her know how serious I was about her staying in contact with me. Even though I didn't care for the nigga, I could tell he had feelings for my sister and would protect her. I still wanted to catch a fade with his cocky ass, though. His attitude was almost as rude as mine, so I knew we would eventually butt heads if he was around long enough.

"Thank you, thank you! I love you, Elijah Raheem," she gushed while hugging me tight.

"I love you too, Greedy," I replied as I hugged her back as tight as I could. Was too geeked to have my sister back in my life and be able to get hugs like this again. Both she and Dakota were my heart and the only ones I really showed any love or affection. Others rarely if ever saw this side of me, and that's exactly how I wanted it.

I released my sister from my hold just as the garage door started going up. Rio pulled out in a clean-ass black Mercedes-Benz G-Class SUV. The nigga was still mugging as he pulled up next to us. I high key wanted to punch him in his fucking face or shoot him in both of his gotdamn kneecaps, leaving his ass immobile.

"I'll call you later, okay?" Breelyn said after kissing my cheek.

"You better," I told her before addressing Rio. "Say, man, I'ma say this once and be done with it. I'm trusting you with my baby sister. You fuck with her or let someone else fuck with her, and I'm on yo' ass, ya dig?"

"Fuck outta here with that weak-ass threat. If you thought I was gon' do something to her or let some fuck shit happen to her, you wouldn't be leaving her here with me. So kill that shit," he scoffed before rolling his window up without further acknowledging me.

See what I was saying? The nigga was hella disrespectful. "Breelyn, I swear I don't like that fool," I spat.

"I don't see why not. Y'all act just alike," she teased while backing away.

"Whatever, man. If I don't get a text from you within the next hour I'm coming back and dragging your ass away from here," I warned.

"Let's go, Greedy!" dude shouted from the car. Fool rolled his window back down just to say that shit, so I knew he was trying to be funny. Promise I heard his punk ass laugh when he said it. I was the only one who called my sister by that name. No bullshit, I was ready to pull him out of his whip and beat his ass.

"I hear you, brother. I'll talk to you in a little bit." Breelyn rushed to the passenger side when she saw me move toward the truck. She already knew I was at my limit with her punk-ass boyfriend or whatever the fuck he was to her. After waiting for them to pull away, I finally left and headed toward my neck of the woods.

Back in Dallas, I went straight to G's upscale lounge, Good Life. My war-ready attire didn't quite meet the dress-code requirements, but because the place was owned by my best friend, his people knew to let me fall through anyway. I mobbed straight up to my reserved area and kicked back, knowing my bottle of D'Ussé XO was already on the way over to my section.

Swore I loved this place. Everything up in this bitch was extravagant, from the décor to the women. The food was bomb, and the drinks were on point. This spot definitely lived up to its name. Being here reminded me of the good life I was living and the many perks that came with it. I had more money than I'd ever be able to spend, and at this point, I was tired of ripping and running the streets. Was blessed to have made my exit from the game before my luck ran out.

I was trying to get up on some shit like this. Who better to learn from than my boy Giannis? I was constantly reading and doing research after our weekly meetings, so it wouldn't be long before I was owning more than the few washeterias and rental properties I already had. G and I went way back to the sandbox, and he'd stayed down like four flats from day one. He was trill as fuck, but a lot of niggas used to come at him sideways because they thought he was weak and not down enough. Don't let the light skin and good looks fool you. That fool was far from pussy and had some nice-ass hands. Plus, he wasn't afraid to bust his gun.

G had a few other spots that, from the outside looking in, were more my speed. Contrary to popular belief, this here thug liked the finer things in life. If I were to hang out at his booty club Sensations, I was bound to get into it with one of the hating-ass niggas who frequented the establishment. It had happened more times than I could remember. Niggas grilling me because the ladies flocked to a real one while I popped bottles, made it rain, and minded my own business in VIP.

I didn't know who raised these niggas, but I could never understand a grown-ass man hating on the next instead of taking notes and using my balling ass as motivation to do better. Better yet, "git up, git out and git something," like Outkast said in '94. Now don't get it fucked up. I wasn't one of those niggas who got money and felt they were too good and forgot where they came from. I was with that ghetto shit as well. Loved everything about my hood and loved my people even more, but the older I got, the more I thought about the choices I made and what I wanted for my future.

With the changes I was trying to make, I couldn't take a chance of flying off the handle when disrespected by another black man for no other reason than the fact that I had more money or bitches than him. I could admit that I was hotheaded and quick to get out of my hookup.

It was no secret that I didn't take kindly to impudence of any kind from anyone. That's why I didn't like that nigga Rio. Should have shot his ass when I had the chance. Breelyn would never have forgiven me if I'd done that shit, though. She better be grateful I loved her ass.

As promised, she'd texted my phone twice, letting me know she was good. I was about to nut the hell up and drive back out there when she informed me she was spending the night out there with ol' boy. I was only three years older than her and Kota, but I hated the fact that they were having sex. If it were left up to me, they would have remained pure forever.

As for me, I did what the fuck I wanted, when I fucking wanted, with whom I fucking wanted. Didn't have a steady girl in my life and didn't plan to have one in the future, but I did have a few females I dealt with more than others. Dakota often told me that she believed not having my mother in my life hindered me from being able to show women the love they wanted and needed, so that's why I shied away from that aspect of relationships, focusing only on the physical. She could have been right, but who the fuck knows? Her ass ain't no psychologist, so how was she gon' tell me?

I had some memories of my mother, who passed away when I was three years old. Breelyn literally had the same face as our mother, and I believed that's why my father chose let her go live with my Aunt Syl and Uncle Kasey not long after my mother passed. He didn't take her death well and couldn't take looking into Breelyn's face every day. He was still there for us physically and financially, but emotionally he checked out after losing the love of his life to a brain aneurysm. I remained in the home with him as I grew up, but I spent a lot of time at Dakota's so that I could be close to her and my sister.

My father pretty much let me do what I wanted. I was the kid nobody could tell shit. I had no curfew, so I ripped and ran the streets as much as my dad did. Drinking and smoking weed right along with him until a serious health scare a few years back caused me to ease up on that shit. After a while, not even my pops could handle me. Uncle Kasey was the only person who could get through to me. It was because of him I was still breathing and had never been incarcerated. He was the only one to discipline me and show me tough love, and I respected him. He'd beaten the brakes off me plenty of times, so I knew not to try him. Uncle Kase was the reason that Dakota was so hard. Unc taught her not to put up with bullshit from anyone. Surprised the hell out of me when she dealt with that foolish-ass nigga, Montell, for as long as she did. Still, I didn't worry about her as much as I worried about Greedy.

Just like he did with Breelyn, Pops threw money at me as a way of showing love, but that's not what we needed. We needed him, but he wasn't available to us. Not emotionally anyway. Because of him, I never wanted to procreate or love a woman that deeply. So deep that without her you're like, "Fuck the world and everyone in it," including your seeds. Nah, no thanks. Swore that nigga was no more good after she left us. Never told us he loved us, but I guessed he had to since he was still around. After she passed, he could have just dipped on us all together, but he didn't, so that had to count for something. At least that's the way I saw it. It was no wonder my baby sister fell into that situation with David. She was out here looking for the love of her own father. Uncle Kasey was there for her, but to have your biological father alive, living in the same city, and have him not be there for you had to fuck her up just a little. I guessed that shit messed with me too, but I was a man, so I handled it a bit different.

On the cool, I wanted what my nigga G had with my cousin. You could just look at them and tell that they loved each other. I was a thug-ass nigga, but like any other human being, I wanted to love and be loved by someone. I just didn't know how so I didn't bother. Definitely didn't want to hurt someone I cared about due to my internal struggles. Maybe love would find me one day, but until then I was on the hunt for that new pussy.

As I sipped my drink, my eyes scanned the building, trying to see if I could find a female worthy of receiving this dick tonight. I was in desperate need of some stress relief. I had to do a double take when I spotted the face of a familiar female caking with some suit-and-tie nigga at the bar. Dude wasn't even her type, and she knew it. It had been months since we ended things, and she seemed to have moved on from me with no problems. If I were to ever settle down with anyone she would have been the one. I wasn't on that shit, though, and she got tired of waiting for me to come around, so she cut me off. I would never tell a soul, but that shit hurt. In the end, I couldn't do shit but respect the fact that she wasn't willing to settle for the sex without commitment that I offered the rest of these hoes. Not being able to be out in the open with our shit was another issue she had. She refused to go out like that, and it was one of the reasons I fucked with her so tough.

I was getting uncomfortable with how close she was with dude, though. It was apparent, based on their interaction, that a sexual relationship existed between them, and that had me irritated as fuck. That was supposed to be my pussy. The fact that she was looking good as hell didn't help my mood either. Wearing a long-sleeved white bodysuit with a tight nude pencil skirt and red platform pumps, she looked like perfection. Body was stupid fine and stacked the fuck up. Besides the matte red lipstick, her cocoa brown face was bare and flawless, just the way I liked.

What I couldn't figure out was why she thought it was cool to bring her nigga to a spot that she knew I frequented. I mean she rode my dick numerous times on this same red leather sofa I was lounging on right now, so she knew what was up. I guessed today was Disrespect Rah Day and I had yet to receive the fucking memo. This shit here was the last straw, though, and had me about to blow a fucking gasket. I decided I would give her a chance to set things straight before I went the fuck off. I quickly shot her a text and watched her to see her reaction.

Me: You gotta be fucking crazy coming in here with that nigga. You must want him to die tonight.

I know, it was a bit extreme, but as you can tell I ain't wrapped too tight. And I meant that shit so fuck it. A few seconds passed before she picked her phone up off the bar and looked at the screen. Eyes wide, she looked around until she finally found me standing over the railing of my section, glaring at her. She had the nerve to be glaring right back at me like, "Nigga, what?" We maintained eye contact until dude gently touched her elbow and started talking. Guessed the nigga was asking if she was okay. She only nodded and accepted a forehead kiss from him. After messing with her phone for a moment, she placed it face down on the bar, but I received no response. I knew damn well she didn't delete my message. She must have thought I was playing.

Me: Yo, if I have to come down there, I'ma shoot that nigga in his muthafuckin' face.

Me: Send his ass home and meet me at the spot.

I was giving her ass thirty fucking seconds to either respond or get the fuck out of here with that nigga she was clinging to. She knew me well enough to know I wouldn't hesitate to come downstairs and fuck their entire night up. Her bigheaded ass had the audacity to roll her eyes as she read the second text and angrily began typing. I couldn't help but laugh at her reaction.

TheOne: He's leaving, but I'll be going with him and I ain't meeting your ass nowhere!

My jaw clenched when she placed her phone in her purse then wrapped her arms around dude's neck before whispering something in his ear. Clearly, he was pleased with what she was saying, by the goofy-ass look on his face. I, however, was anything but pleased and felt like she was taking shit too far.

That was all I needed to see before I headed that way. I knew she deserved to move on with someone else since I couldn't give her what she needed. I just didn't want to have a ring-side seat to the action. Didn't even want to hear about her fucking around with anyone else. Her shaky ass saw me coming, so she grabbed ol' boy's hand and moved through the crowd toward the exit. It was too late for that shit. Her first violation was bringing the nigga in here. Then she hugged up on his ass knowing I was watching, and she had the nerve to talk shit about it. Whatever happened to that nigga tonight was going to be on her. Should've known not to play with me like that.

When I made it to the bottom of the stairs leading to my section, I was cut off by Kiara's ho ass. I knew I was playing with fire when I hit this psycho-ass girl off. It happened once, and I hadn't dipped back since, but it wasn't because she wasn't throwing it at me. I just wasn't interested. She was a beautiful plus-sized woman, but the pussy was straight garbage, and she was crazy as fuck on top of all that. Chubby girls and crazy hoes usually have the best pussy, but that was not the case with her. I wanted nothing to do with this bird, but she couldn't get it through her head. Kiara was one of Giannis's hostesses, and he'd warned me that she was clingy. He told me not to go there, but my hard-headed ass ain't listen. Now every time I came through here she stayed in my face or cock blocked when other females tried to get at me.

"Goddamn, are you retarded or what?" I snapped. Bitch had to be off her rocker to keep trying me like this, and right now I had no time to entertain her lunatic ass. She was cute as hell, but this stalker shit made her so unattractive.

"You are so damn rude," she said with what she thought was a sexy smile. Bitch was acting like I didn't just curb her ass. "What you got up for later?" she asked while pulling at the bottom of my black thermal.

"Whatever it is, yo' nappy-headed ass won't be involved," I spat before pushing past her. I could hear her talking shit as I walked away, but I didn't have time to check her. If she kept that shit up, I was gon' get her ass fired, or better yet I could murk her looney ass and end all problems I had with her. My boy would be pissed because she was good at her job, but he would just have to get over that shit. Bitch was getting on my last nerve.

By the time I made it to the bar ol' girl was long gone. Gun in hand, I rushed outside and scanned the parking lot, but they were nowhere in sight. They got ghost quick as fuck. At this point, I didn't even want to go back inside. The chill mood I was trying to get to no longer seemed to be within reach. My day had started fucked up and had ended the same way. *Might as well take my ass home and try again tomorrow.*

On the ride to my place, my mind was consumed with thoughts of her and what she was going to be doing with dude tonight, and that shit caused some unfamiliar pressure within my chest. I had to shake this shit off, because I didn't like the way I was feeling. She would be with me if I weren't so fucked up in the head, but in my heart, I knew I wasn't what she needed right now. Hell, by the time I got my shit together, her ass was probably going to be married with two and a half kids and a damn dog. The visualization itself made me cringe.

When I made it to my crib, I headed straight for the shower, hoping that would help me relax. What I needed was a shot of D'Ussé and some good pussy to ease my mind, but I was in for the night. Getting a room was out of the question, and inviting someone to my spot was not something I made a habit of. With every showerhead aimed at me, the hot water began to soothe my body and release the built-up tension.

After another fifteen minutes, I was squeaky clean and smelling of that Dove bodywash that the ladies loved so much. Sitting at the edge of the bed, wearing nothing but a towel around my waist, I picked up my phone to see if ol' girl had hit me back. Wasn't too surprised to see that she hadn't.

As soon as I placed my phone back on the bedside table, someone rang my doorbell. A smile crept across my face at the sound. It had to be her. She was the only one besides my family and G who knew where I lived. Looking through the peephole, my suspicions were confirmed. Still wearing only a towel and no longer smiling, I pulled the door open. Couldn't let her see how much her presence pleased me.

"So is that how you're going to act every time you see me out with someone, Elijah?" she asked with her hand on her ample hips. Face all scrunched up with fire in her eyes while she called herself trying to check me. I saw the lust and appreciation in her eyes as well as she eyed my damp body.

I didn't respond as my eyes traveled the length of her body, not missing a single curve. Swore it didn't make sense for her body to be that fucking crazy. Grabbing her by the back of her neck, I pulled her into my place and locked the door. I expected a little resistance when I crashed my lips against hers, but I didn't get any. If anything, she was more into the kiss than I was.

Her hand went to the towel, and in one swift motion she yanked it from my body and dropped to her knees. Looked like I was about to get that stress relief after all. And who better to bless me than my favorite girl? Dakota and Breelyn would probably fuck me up if they knew I was creeping with this girl, but I couldn't help it, and I didn't want to. I knew all about that bullshit in her past, and I didn't judge her or hold it against her. Like I said before, if I was going to settle down with anyone it would be her, and I didn't give a damn what anyone had to say about it.

Chapter 14

Rio

A Not-so-classy Affair

Swore I didn't want to bring Breelyn with me tonight, but my baby insisted on tagging along. I normally worked solo, but when I saw how enraged she became when she learned about what was happening to these innocent children, I had no choice but to let her in on at least the first part of my plan. Plus, she had the plug on the tickets, so I didn't have to sneak up in that bitch like I'd originally planned.

After calling and apologizing to Chino for ditching him at the zoo, the fool forgave her and made her promise that she would still be his guest at the ball. My gut was telling me that the fool had ulterior motives for wanting her there,

but whatever he had in mind would never happen. Had to bite my tongue the entire time she
was on the phone with him. I knew she was only
faking interest for the benefit of what needed
to be done, but it was still hard listening to her
sweet-talk the nigga. Told him instead of Dakota
she was bringing her male cousin who was new
to town and looking to meet some women. I
couldn't believe he actually bought the story
she fed him about vomiting and messing up her
clothes at the zoo and being too ashamed to face
him afterward. She lied to him, saying she had
Dakota come get her because she didn't want
him to see her in the shape she was in. Dumb-ass
nigga. No way would I have believed that story if
she came at me with that shit.

"Damn, Breelyn, you looking good as hell,
mama." I almost gasped when she finally emerged
from the restroom, wearing the black strapless,
ankle-length lace dress. Baby was gorgeous, and
I couldn't even describe how happy I was to call
her my own.

Yes, mine! As soon as we finished dinner last
night, we talked, and it was established that we
were together. An official couple. I didn't want
there to be any confusion about where I wanted
this thing between us to go. Couldn't have my
lady out there wondering what we were or ques-

tioning my feelings for her, so I laid it all out for her and told her exactly what I needed from her and how much I cared about her. I was just glad that she felt the same way. I wasn't a lying-ass nigga, so I even told her what I did for a living and my reason for doing it. Was surprised when she accepted it and told me she was rocking with me either way.

"Thank you, baby. You look mighty dapper yourself," she complimented me, brushing a piece of lint from the sleeve of my tux before snaking her arms around my neck.

"I'm kind of salty that other niggas get to see you in this bad-ass dress, though," I admitted as I palmed her ass, pulling her farther into me. Her blond bob was styled to perfection with bouncy curls, and her makeup was light and simple as usual. Seeing her looking this sexy had my dick rising, but we didn't have time to do any of the nasty shit currently floating around in my head. Tonight I had a job to do, so I had to get my head together. I was praying that I could stay focused and not let her being there distract me. Her only task was to get us in, and I would handle the rest. Didn't need her to lead Chino to me or anything. I would never put her in harm's way like that.

"No need to be salty when you know that all of this belongs to you and only you," my baby said before blessing me with a sensual kiss. That shit shut me right on up.

"Good. You remember the plan, right? All you're doing is getting us in, and I'll take it from there. Deviating from that plan in any way might potentially delay me from doing what I need to do," I stressed to her.

"I understand, DeMario. Chino needs to be dealt with, so I would never do anything to get in the way of that," she assured me. I just hoped she could keep her word and not try to get herself more involved than she already was.

Upon arrival to the ball, my girl and I put our game faces on and went our separate ways. She went off to find Chino as I took on the role of her cousin who'd just arrived in town, looking for a few lady friends to help me get acquainted with my new surroundings. As discussed, she played Chino close while I made my rounds.

In order to stay focused, I had to block out the fact that Breelyn was in the building. We didn't even plan to leave together tonight. In about an hour she would slip away, telling Chino she was going to the ladies' room, when in fact Dakota would be waiting at the side exit we'd scoped out days earlier to take her home.

Once she was out of the way, I could do my thing, and afterward, I would pick her up from Kota's place.

I wasn't joking when I told Breelyn that I planned to kill every person here who was involved with the trafficking ring Chino headed. The problem was way bigger than this circle, but I figured I could at least take a small portion of these sick bastards out and save a few children in the process. First thing I had to do was get a hold of the list showing everyone invited tonight. In the coming weeks, I could investigate to see who was involved and who was just here thinking they were doing something good for the children.

When the time came to see if I could get my hands on the list, I didn't even have to turn on the charm to get what I needed. Before I could approach her, the thirsty-ass event coordinator was all in my grill, hinting that she wanted to suck me off. Baby was a beautiful chocolate chick with striking features, but she was doing the absolute most to have just met a nigga tonight. Instead of doing her damn job, she was falling right into my trap.

After agreeing to let her do her thing, I followed her to a room in back, checking my surroundings as I moved along. I walked in behind her, into a small but neat office space, and I watched her place onto a desk the folder and clipboard she'd been holding. She pulled out a hair tie to pull her hair back. Bitch was ready rock steady. Guessed she did shit like this on the regular.

I didn't even give her a chance to turn around to face me before I had her ass in a sleeper hold. I'd performed the move so many times that she was out of it within seconds. Didn't want to kill her, just needed her out of the way while I took screenshots of the guest list before moving on to my target. Bitch was gon' be looking crazy as hell when they found her in here passed out on the floor. I would have loved to stick around to hear what explanation she would give. It wasn't like she could tell her boss that she was about to suck the dick of a man she had met only twenty minutes before but he ended up choking her out instead. Hilarious. I didn't have time for that, though. I had a little under ten minutes before Dakota was due to be here to get Breelyn, so I needed to get a move on.

After getting what I needed from the paper-work, I made my way back to the party, hoping to lay eyes on Breelyn's fine ass before she left. I watched as she excused herself from Chino but not before he kissed her temple. Seeing that shit had me adjusting my fucking collar.

Shit felt tight as hell all of a sudden, knowing anything on his filthy-ass body touched mine. Mine as in hers, that is. Seemed my girl was just as repulsed by it as I was. If she had rolled her eyes any harder, them shits would have been permanently fixed in the back of her head. Could tell that him putting his lips on her struck a nerve, and her response to it caused a chuckle to slip from mine. After tonight my baby wouldn't have to worry her pretty little head about his ass again.

She didn't see me, but I watched her closely as her body moved sensually through the crowd. Her walk was naturally sexy as hell. Booty rocking every-fucking-where. Shat! She wasn't even trying and was easily the baddest female in the building. I was a little biased, but I ain't give a fuck. My girl was the shit.

I had to admit that I was proud of how Breelyn carried herself tonight. I stuck to the script, doing plenty of flirting, and she never once broke character when she was close enough to me to witness it. And although she had a role to play as well, she was never over the top or disrespectful in her show of affection toward Chino. Had she done the opposite, I wasn't sure I would have been able to manage as well as she had. Probably would have snatched his ho ass up and murked him in front of everyone here, but my baby made sure not to do anything to send me over the edge. She already knew I was muthafuckin' certified. Ask about me.

I looked on as Chino checked his watch then glanced toward the corridor that led to the restrooms in search of Breelyn. Nigga's jaw was clenched in irritation as he made small talk and half listened to the people surrounding him. He was lucky my lady was no longer in the building, because had any of that aggression been directed toward her, his death would have been more painful than what I originally had planned for his ass.

After ten or so minutes he had enough of the waiting game and made his way toward the ladies' room. It was about damn time. I needed to finish up here before someone discovered that ho passed out in the office or she woke up on her own. Waiting in the cut at the end of the hallway, I spotted Chino when he emerged from checking the restroom for Breelyn. He had his phone up to his ear, so I decided to listen in for a bit. Figured he might be trying to get in contact with her.

"Man, this bitch is like Houdini or some shit. I don't know if she done somehow caught on to what's up or her ass just likes playing games, but she's gone, and I'm supposed to hand her over to Saldana tonight or else," he whispered into the phone.

The fear in his voice was evident, and I couldn't believe the shit I was hearing. I mean I knew what he was into, but from what I'd gathered, he only dealt in children. Knowing what he had in store for my girl had me hot as fish grease. I recalled seeing the name Saldana on the list, so it was likely he was somewhere in here tonight, but I couldn't deal with him at the moment. He would eventually get his issue, though.

"This is the second time she's got ghost on me right before the exchange, and this nigga already talking about sending his hitters for me, because he think I done fucked him out of his bread and plan to keep her for myself or some shit. No doubt I would have loved to fuck her fine ass at least once before they ruin her ass in Mexico, but the money he dropped for her trumps me getting a nut, you feel me? I'on know what I'ma tell this nigga this time," he stressed.

The more he talked, the angrier I became. I was fucking his entire world up tonight. I was bringing out the snakes, rats, and pit bulls on his ho ass. Looked like Saldana would never have the chance to get his hands on this dirty nigga for not meeting his end of the deal. Chino was all mine and Saldana would see me real soon as well. Good thing he informed whoever he was talking to on the phone of the situation, because they would think it was Saldana's doing when this nigga came up missing.

As soon as he hit that red button on his cell and disconnected the call, I was on his ass. A forceful blow to the back of his head nearly took him down, but the powerful fist to his chin knocked him out instantly. Nigga never saw me coming. Within seconds he was over my shoulder as I moved toward the same exit Breelyn used. Thankfully no one was out in the alley, and I'd shut off the cameras earlier to ensure no one would see my face as we were leaving. The dummy car I picked up yesterday was still parked where I left it, and Chino was placed securely in the trunk. I hopped in and exited the alley slowly before pulling onto the street, en route to the destination of this fuck nigga's final resting place.

Chapter 15

David Parrish

We'll Never End

"David, are you serious right now?" Shawna asked like she didn't hear what the fuck I just said.

"Hell, yeah, I'm serious. Get the fuck out, and I'll be back by the time you're done," I spat.

"Dave, don't you want to find out for yourself what's going on with the baby? You know I'm not going to remember everything the doctor tells me," she reasoned with her eyes becoming cloudy.

Bitch looked like she was about to fall apart at any moment, and I wished she would so I could fuck her ass up in that parking lot. It was her own damn fault she was in this situation. Told her ass to get rid of the baby when we first found out, but no, she just had to keep it. Now she wanted me to be happy about it. Fuck outta here.

"Shawna, this ain't your first baby, so quit acting like you clueless. I'on need to know what the fuck they say anyway. Now if you don't get yo' big ass the fuck up out my whip, we gon' have a problem. And you better wipe yo' face before you walk up in there. Get on my nerves with all that pouting and ho-ass crying," I fumed, looking at her in disgust.

She knew I wasn't playing because she got out without another word, quietly closing the car door. I barely let that bitch close before I pulled off. The defeated look on her face did nothing to move me. At this point my heart was dead, and I didn't give a fuck about much. Not even her or this dumb-ass appointment to check on our daughter she was carrying.

Feeling eyes burning a hole through me, I looked in the rearview mirror to find my son, Davy, staring at me like he wanted to kick my ass. He had his headphones on and had been watching something on his tablet, but I was sure he could tell that his mother and I had been arguing. At seven years old Davy was a smart kid, so I tried my best not to show this side of myself in front of him, but he knew better.

I could tell by the way he was glaring at me. His ass had better bump it down before he got fucked up trying to stick up for his mama. I loved my boy, but I wouldn't tolerate any disrespect from him.

My life could not possibly get more fucked up than it was right now. My shit was in utter fucking shambles and had been ever since my girl walked out on me last year. My ass had been blowing Breelyn's phone up and following her around since she'd returned to Dallas, but I had yet to make my presence known. I'd been biding my time and waiting for the right time to approach her, and our first encounter hadn't gone anything like I planned.

I had taken the day off from stalking her, so I couldn't believe my luck or my eyes when I stepped off the escalator in the galleria and spotted Breelyn moving in my direction. My girl was so beautiful it was crazy. What surprised me, though, was the way she straight chumped me off when I asked for her number. Talked to me like I wasn't shit, and it took everything in me not to bust her in her gotdamn mouth in front of all those people.

After all I'd done for her, and she was just like, "Fuck you." I just knew that when she saw a nigga, she was gon' get some act right. Hell, that's why she fled the state in the first place. She knew she wouldn't be able to stay away from me if she remained in Dallas. I still had no idea where she was all that time, but I was lucky enough to get her number from a friend of the family. In fact, it was the same person who told me Breelyn was back in town.

After being gone for over a year, my baby looked at me like I was a stranger who had never meant a thing to her, and that hurt my heart. Her ass was probably just showing out because that bitch Dakota was nearby. I couldn't stand that little muthafucka there, and she felt the same way about me. Believe it or not, I tried spitting game to Kota first when I ran into them at Rochester Park one Sunday afternoon. Couldn't believe it when that bitch curbed me. I quickly found that Breelyn was the better choice anyway. She was submissive and someone I knew I could mold into the woman I needed her to be.

Dakota's ass was a live wire, always bucking the system and challenging Montell. His weak ass let her get away with murder, but that shit wouldn't have worked for me. In the beginning, it used to piss me off when Montell would brag about what a freak she was and how wet and bomb the pussy was. In some ways, I felt like it was me who was supposed to be experiencing her that way, but I would forever keep that shit to myself. I already knew Montell's lovesick ass would die if he ever found out. My only solution was to behave as if I hated her, and eventually I came to feel that way. Hated her ass for rejecting me and also for turning Breelyn against me.

She was always telling my lady what to do and saying what was best for her. Quick to jump in a nigga's face, too, but if I were to knock her ass out she would think I did her wrong, or she'd run to get that nigga Rah like he was somebody to fear. I mean I knew Rah was with the shits or whatever, but so was I, and I feared no man. We'd exchanged words a few times, but when he came at me about hitting his sister, it turned physical. If I weren't so drunk and high, I was sure he wouldn't have gotten the best of me. After that incident, I told Breelyn that it was either me or him, and she chose right. I'd succeeded in turning Breelyn against her brother, but Dakota was someone she just wouldn't turn on. Not even for me. And, trust me, I'd tried.

As I made my way to west Dallas to check in with my man who I had tailing Breelyn, I was trying to recall at what point things started spiraling out of control in my relationship with Breelyn. When we met, she was like a breath of fresh air, all innocent and inexperienced. I was her first everything, and she literally worshipped the ground I walked on. She was everything to me for the first few years, but after finding out that I wouldn't have a career in the NFL, I turned to the streets, and she no longer fit into the lifestyle I was living.

I was much too selfish to let her go, though. Dakota, on the other hand, would have been the perfect woman for a hustler, but that's neither here nor there. With the money I was making the women were plenty, and I indulged every chance I got. My cheating led to Breelyn bitching and leaving me every other week. I continued to step outside of our relationship, and although I knew she wouldn't leave permanently, the threats she made of finding a nigga who would treat her better resulted in me choking her ass out more than once.

Because I was doing her so dirty, my mind often played tricks on me with thoughts of her fucking around on me. Didn't even want to imagine my baby giving her body to the next man, but for some reason, I just couldn't leave them hoes alone and be true to her. Sex with different women became a real addiction of mine. It got so bad that Breelyn just stopped nagging me about it. She stopped checking my phone, stopped confronting me when I walked in the house at six a.m., and no longer questioned me about my relationship with my baby mama.

That should have been the first clue that she was done. Instead of taking heed, a nigga got the big head and tried to be on some pimp shit. At the time I thought that her not nagging me meant that she'd finally accepted my ways, so I didn't feel the need to sneak around anymore. I wanted all my women to know about one another and be okay with me having them all. I honestly thought that Breelyn knew what we had was real. I loved her and sex with other women was just that, sex.

Y'all might think I was crazy, but my goal was to have both my side bitches moved in by the end of the year. Shawna was down with the movement off the muscle but Breelyn, who I considered my main, wasn't having it, so she moved out. It took some mind games, but she finally came home and accepted Shawna and my son living in the same house as us. There was an adjustment period, but things seemed to be going smoothly for a minute. If I'd known that Breelyn would really leave, like leave and not just go back to her aunt's house for a week or two, I would have left well enough alone. It would have been nothing for me to keep fucking my baby mama and that other ho on the side, and Breelyn would have been none the wiser, but that just wasn't enough for me.

Around the time that all this shit popped off, I'd begun snorting cocaine more than just every now and then or when I was partying. The shit had become a daily habit and was beginning to affect my thinking. Had I been in my right mind, I would have realized that moving Shawna in was pushing it, but I was determined to have my cake and eat it, too. A nigga was trying to have nightly foursomes up in that bitch. Unfortunately, that stupid move cost me Breelyn. The only chick I'd ever loved out of them all.

Shit was all bad now because Shawna's ass was pregnant again, and I was sure Breelyn somehow found out. My baby loved Davy, but I doubted she would accept another child. She had the game fucked up, though, if she thought it was over between us. We would never end, and that was all there was to it. I'd given her a whole fucking year to get her mind right, but time was up, and she needed to get prepared to bring her ass home.

Yeah, I knew I messed up, but she owed me a chance to fix things. It was me who provided for her and kept her laced with the finer things for years. Clothes, money, jewelry, and she stayed driving a fresh-ass whip. All courtesy of me. She only got that little cooking job to teach me a lesson, and I let her keep it because her working gave me more time to run the streets and fuck other females. Played that shit smooth, too. Had her thinking I was digging her growing independence and ability to bring money in when all the while I was doing my thing.

All of that was in the past, and I was determined to make things right. First thing I needed was to get rid of Shawna, and second was to shake these fucking drugs then try to get back on somehow. Nobody was really fucking with me because word was out that I had fallen off and was using. I'd even lost my connect due to coming up short on his bread one too many times. My ass would have been six feet under had my cousin Montell not helped me rob that nigga Renzo from the east side. I used the money from that caper to pay Tonio back before that deadline. He ended up cutting ties with me after that. Said he had too much love for me to end up having to kill me over some money. I still had my home and cars, but my money was looking hella funny.

Once I got my rider back on my team, I felt like everything else would fall into place. If Breelyn didn't see things my way, then we were going to have a problem. If I couldn't be with her, then no one would, and that's just what that was. If she thought it was over, she had another think coming. Handling Dakota would get me closer to my goal, so that's what I planned to do first.

"What you got for me, my nigga?" I asked when I finally pulled up on Brent in the parking lot of Wimpy's on Singleton. He was some flunky nigga who was doing my dirty work and stalking Breelyn while I ran Shawna to her appointment.

"Not much, big dawg. I lost her about ten minutes after I started following her. I tried to call you, but you ain't pick up," he answered slowly, looking high out of his mind.

"Man, I told yo' retarded ass that I had to run my baby mama to the doctor. How the hell you lose her that fast?" I asked in annoyance. Guessed if I wanted a job done, I'd have to do it myself. This slow-ass nigga clearly wasn't up for it, and if he thought he was getting paid, he had another think coming.

"The nigga who was driving was on some Dale Earnhardt Jr. shit. Turning corners and speeding like a damn fool. I kept up the best I could, but the nigga finally shook me," he reported.

"That was probably her brother. Breelyn ain't crazy enough to be riding around my city with some other nigga," I reasoned. "I'll hit you if I need you again."

I pulled off before he could respond, because I didn't need him asking for some money he would never see. Nigga couldn't even keep up with his target for a full fifteen minutes, so he hadn't earned shit anyhow. I ended up pulling up to the doctor's office right as Shawna was walking out.

"Everything is great with our princess." Shawna beamed, hopping back in the car.

I didn't even bother responding to her. She was happy and grinning again like I hadn't checked her ass over an hour ago. Even Davy was in the back, shaking his head at his mother. Bitch was dingy as fuck. I treated this woman like shit and had tried everything to get her to leave, but she just wouldn't let go. Honestly, Shawna was a good woman and had been down for me for years. Her only fault was that she wasn't Breelyn. *Her ass might end up having to get dealt with right along with Kota.*

Chapter 16

Dakota

Litty Again

An entire year since my last release and I had finally put out another book. My small team of writers all had books out that were doing exceptionally well, and now it was my time to shine. I'd put my writing on hold to focus on my growing business, so it felt good to get back to it. I probably would have waited until next year to work on another project, but Giannis wasn't having that. It was his encouragement that pushed me to get it done, and once I got going again, I felt so good and was happy to be doing what I loved. I owed that all to my man. I still handled business for my team, but he made me promise to set aside a couple of hours every day to work on my book.

After only three months the latest Kota B book was complete. It would be a three-part series, and I was almost done writing the second installment. I was so excited and ready for everyone to read my latest ghetto love story that I could hardly contain myself. No one was more excited and proud than Mr. Giannis Williams, though. This book release event was all his doing. It was being held at his lounge, Good Life. I loved that my baby was so supportive of me and my work, and I tried my hardest to be that for him as well.

Tonight for instance. Although I was tired of folk interrupting us, asking for instructions, and tearing him away from me for long periods of time, I recognized he was working so I let him make it. His staff was A1, so he usually didn't have to be so hands-on, but I knew it was his way of making sure everything was right for tonight. For me. As always he went above and beyond to make sure I was happy. The book signing, which was held here as well, ended hours ago and it was amazing. My crazy-ass family along with a host of associates and fans came out to show love, and I'd been on a natural high all day. Right now though, the place was lit, and it was time for the fucking turn up.

While I waited for Giannis to return I danced my ass off, got my drink on, and cut up with

Breelyn and Mel. I was too cute tonight if I did say so myself. My silk press was on point, makeup was flawless, and the sleeveless printed mini dress by Alice + Olivia I was rocking had me feeling super sexy. Olive green ankle-strap heels graced my feet, showing off my cute pedicured toes. Of course, my girls were looking just as cute and seemed to be having the time of their lives as well.

"So, Ms. Melanie, what's going on with that?" I asked while nodding toward her man.

She glanced over at him briefly before turning back toward us. "He's cool or whatever. We've been kicking it for a li'l minute, and the sex is bomb." She shrugged.

"But?" I prodded, because it seemed like she wanted to say more. Just because I didn't like to share my business didn't mean my ass wasn't nosy as hell when it came to other folks and their tea. I drank that shit ice cold with three sugars and a lemon wedge. Fuck what you heard.

"I don't know, Kota. Just feels like something is missing. I feel like shit for even complaining because he's such a good dude and we get along so well. My folks fucking love him. I'm sure there are plenty of bitches who would kill to have a faithful, successful, attractive man like him, and here I am wondering, 'what if?' Like, is this really it for me? As good as it gets?" she questioned with a far-off look in her eyes.

"You still thinking about ol' boy?" I said, shaking my head. Before Mel's newest fling she was with some other guy for about two years. According to her, it was a complicated situation, which was why we never met him. Although she neither confirmed nor denied it, Breelyn and I assumed he was married or in a relationship and that's why she'd never brought him around, but I could tell she cared a lot about him. She didn't seem like the type to play side chick, but you never knew, and she surely wasn't giving up all the details.

"Naw, that shit been dead. I'm just saying how I feel," she said with a wave of her hand while glancing back at her man once more.

He was in deep conversation with Rio, but it was like he felt her watching and looked up to offer her a wink and smile. She gave him a shy smile while tucking her hair behind her ear. It was the cutest thing. Also sad, because if you sat back and watched them interact it was obvious that he was way more into her than she was him. That had to be tough. Being with someone who liked you more or possibly even loved you when your feelings were nowhere near that level had to make her feel bad. I didn't necessarily believe her when she said she was over her last guy, either.

I was about to comment further, until I peeped my man making his rounds. Baby was mobbing through the crowd like the boss he was, turning down the advances of numerous groupies and gold diggers all while regulating and greeting the crowd with that winning smile. Giannis was fine as fuck and was all business at the moment. I couldn't take my eyes off of him as he finally made his way back to our closed-off section upstairs after stepping away for the umpteenth time tonight.

"You straight?" He stared down at me lovingly.

"Yes, I'm straight, honey. Thank you again for all of this. Because of you, this day has been amazing," I said with a soft kiss to his lips.

"You're welcome, love. You know I'd do anything to make you happy, right?" he said, still gazing into my light browns.

"I know, and I love you for that," I replied shyly.

"I love you too, ma," he told me. Before we could kiss again like planned, one of his employees spoke into his earpiece.

While he walked off to the side, handling business, I stared at him like a lovesick teen. Sometimes I felt this man was just too good to be true. So far no side bitches had popped out, no side babies, or any of the other drama I had become accustomed to in my last situation. Fuck shit had become the norm, so a bitch was still adjusting to being in a healthy, loving relationship. It was a shame that I had to get used to being treated so well by a man.

Once he was back at my side, we shared a steamy kiss before joining our family and friends for the festivities. I sat on his lap for the next hour, swaying to the music. My baby was able to get DJ KO out of Oklahoma City to come through for the event. We met in college, and this brother was smart, good-looking, and knew how to keep any party crunk. Whether it was a club, a hood-ass house party, or a classy affair, dude did his thing. Like right now he had this bitch rocking while we were all boo'd up having the time of our lives.

As I continued to twerk in Giannis's lap, Breelyn was standing against the balcony railing, overlooking the dance floor with Rio hugging up on her from behind. Mel was snuggled up with her guy while Rah had two baddies, one on each side of him. Beautiful, classy-looking women, too. Only Rah's crazy ass could get away with some shit like that. These hoes were loony tunes behind him, and this was a prime example. I couldn't do shit but shake my head and laugh, looking forward to the day he settled down.

Even Giannis's cousin Jahshua came out for the occasion and brought along his beautiful wife, Camryi. He stayed snuggled up under her, kissing her neck and whispering to her. Her ass hadn't stopped smiling since they arrived. They were the cutest couple, and it was obvious that the love was real between the two. The kind of black love I wrote about in my books was present in abundance tonight, and I loved every minute of it. Giannis had a photographer up here with us who took pictures throughout the night, and I couldn't wait to see them.

"Who the fuck invited this bitch?"

I perked up when I heard the irritation in Breelyn's voice. Giannis had just stepped away to take care of something, so I wasted no time jumping up to see who my cousin was talking about. "What bitch?" I asked, coming to stand by her side as she explained to Rio what was going on and who was who.

Lo and behold, it was none other than Jada. She was dumb as hell and thought we were still cool, so I wasn't too shocked to see her here, but what had my face screwed up was the sight of the two men who walked up to her and began caking with her at the bar. With Jada coming around like she was, I knew she had a hidden agenda, but if I found out that it involved either of them, I was gon' whip her ass. Straight up.

"Who y'all bitches over here plotting on?" Mel asked as she came to post up with us.

We were too busy mugging Jada to answer, so she just followed our eyes down. When hers landed on our enemy her face was just as screwed up as ours. Her reaction was strange, because I wasn't aware of them having any beef or even knowing each other. She was probably just on some petty shit and didn't like her because she knew we didn't. Her issue might not have even been with Jada. Could be she was just upset that David and Montell had the balls to show up on my big night.

Just when I made a move to go down there to confront them and ask them to leave my party, the DJ cut the music, and I heard my man's voice on the mic asking for everyone's attention. Temporarily forgetting about our unwanted guests, I focused on Giannis, who now had the spotlight on him. This was one sexy-ass man, y'all, and I couldn't wait to get him up out of that clean-ass suit he was wearing tonight. Loved a man who was able to switch his style up and still look amazing. As we waited for him to continue, flutes of champagne were being passed around by the staff.

"I just want to thank everyone for coming out to celebrate my lady's latest book release. Daily, for the last few months, I was a witness to the work she put in on this one, and I know er'body gon' love it just as much as I do. See, one of the perks of being Dakota's man is that I get to test read all her shit before it comes out, so y'all really in last place," he joked, causing the audience to laugh. "Seriously though, Dakota, baby, I'm so proud of you, and I love you to life. To Kota B!" he said with his glass raised.

"To Kota B!" everyone shouted before drinking to my success as I stared dreamily at my guy.

"Aye, and if you didn't make it out for the book signing earlier today, there's a table adjacent to the picture area that's full of signed copies of the book, T-shirts, coffee mugs, and much more. So please support my baby and purchase some stuff before you leave tonight," he added before handing the mic back to KO, who shouted me out before cranking the music back up.

I didn't even know he had set that up. Now I knew why he had me signing all those extra copies yesterday. I was most definitely breaking his ass off tonight. He wasn't even ready for the freak shit I was going to introduce him to when we got home. I appreciated him, and I was going to show him just how much.

Our eyes were locked as we made our way to each other. When I made it to the bottom of the steps, my view of my dream guy was suddenly cut off by my worst nightmare and the last person I wanted to see. I had forgotten just that fast that he was here.

"Damn, Kota, I wasn't aware that we were seeing other people," Montell said with his brow raised.

"Nigga, are you serious?" I asked with my face screwed up. This man had to be mildly mentally retarded to be in my face with this shit. Seeing other people? Really? I couldn't believe he was still holding on, but I thought, *he had better let that shit go real quick. I fucks with one of the most ignorant men this side of Texas, so him being in my face right now isn't going to end well at all.*

"Hell, yeah! You and I have unfinished business, baby. Fuck this pretty boy come from anyway?" he asked like he had every right to know who the new man in my life was.

Before I could go off on his ass, my people swarmed in from every direction. Giannis stepped between us, causing Montell to damn near fall. Rah stood to the side closest to Montell, and Breelyn was right behind me. Of course, Rio was next to her, waiting for some shit to pop off. I was so glad that my parents and other family had cut out not too long ago, because it would have been a riot up in this bitch. David and this clown in the same room with my family was a recipe for disaster.

"Fuck you in my lady's face for, nigga?" Giannis asked, stepping closer to Montell.

"I'm here showing my support like everyone else, nigga!" Montell answered aggressively.

"Is that right?" my baby questioned as he tugged at his beard with a nod.

Everyone else may have missed it, but I noticed when his hand went behind him to where I knew his gun rested. With my hand wrapping gently around his wrist, he calmed down. Giannis alternated clenching and releasing his fist a few times before I felt it was okay to release him. He was pissed, but I knew he would feel bad tomorrow if he did something tonight that took away from the reason we were here. It was a celebration, and I refused to let Montell ruin it for us.

"That's right," Montell responded confidently, although I could see the nervousness in his eyes and body movement as he stared around at the group of people. He was outnumbered and had allowed his emotions to place him in a fucked-up situation. He didn't know anything about Giannis, so he was probably shook because

Rah was close by. He would never admit it, but he was deathly afraid of my cousin. Hell, most people were. Montell wasn't really about that life, but if he kept fucking around, he would find out that my nigga was the real fucking deal and Elijah Raheem may be the least of his worries when it came to fucking with me.

"Well, I appreciate that shit, but I'm gon' need you to show your support from a distance, fuck nigga. This one here is off-limits to you. She's all me, big fella. But say, if you really want to show your support, buy a book and be sure to leave a review. The shit's really dope," Giannis said, looking Montell up and down and sporting a comical grin. I already knew some silly shit was about to come out of his mouth. "I don't even know how yo' ass made it past the door with yo' granddaddy's suit on anyway. I'ma get on Kiara's ass about that shit. We have a reputation to uphold and you fucking it up, paw paw," he added before turning to face me.

He'd blown Montell off like he was nobody, and it took a lot for me not to laugh at the silly look on my ex's face. Rah and Rio, on the other hand, laughed like that was the funniest shit they'd witnessed in a while. I could tell Montell was embarrassed, and their grown asses didn't make the situation any better. I didn't want to make the man feel bad. I just wanted him to move around and let me be happy with my honey.

"You good, ma?" Giannis asked, pulling me into him by my waist.

"Perfect," I told him as I wrapped my arms around his neck. It was true, too. Tonight was perfect, and so was he. Not flawless perfect but perfect for me. Much like we normally did when we were near one another, we tuned out everyone around us as we pecked away at each other's lips. I squealed when Giannis went down to wrap his arms around my thighs and lift me up into the air, carrying me back up to our section. He was careful not to expose my goodies in the tiny dress I had on. I couldn't stop the bright smile and boisterous laugh that erupted from deep within my belly at his playfulness. Nothing or no one could take away my smile or ruin tonight for me. Not even a bitter ex who had a problem letting go.

Chapter 17

Rio

In the Shadows

We all remained in place, laughing as G's crazy ass rushed up the stairs with Dakota in his arms. That man was a damn fool and would check anyone when it came to his woman. He joked around a lot, but he was quick to pop off. Cursed out a waiter at Ellen's last week for smiling in Kota's face. On the cool, the man was just being polite and doing his job, but G didn't see it that way. Dakota ended up leaving a big-ass tip to make up for his behavior.

I saw when he went to reach for his hammer a moment ago, too. If that wasn't evidence that the nigga was crazy, I didn't know what was. I had no doubt that he would have popped that nigga right here in front of everyone and kept it moving like it wasn't shit. None of us played games when it came to the ladies in our lives, but Giannis always did the extra shit that had everyone laughing.

When Dakota's ex-nigga walked off looking like someone had jacked his dog and his got-damn bike, Rah and I doubled over in even more laughter. I almost felt bad for the man, but he brought it on himself. Some niggas just didn't know when to leave well enough alone. From what I understood about the situation, he'd had a good woman, and he let her get away from him because of his neglect and trifling ways. Plus, the man had a problem hitting women, and y'all already know how I felt about that shit there. When Rah and I noticed we were the only ones still laughing, we made eye contact and mugged the shit out of one another. Just like that, all chuckling ceased, and we were back to normal. As you can see, I still didn't get along with this fool. He had one of the worst attitudes ever, so I stayed fucking with him on GP.

"Babe, I'm going to run to the restroom real quick," Breelyn told me.

"Go ahead. I'll be right here. I need to make a quick phone call anyway," I lied.

From the look on her face, I could tell she wanted me to accompany her, but I wasn't going to offer. My baby was too ashamed to let me know she was still afraid of that nigga David. I could feel the way her body tensed up when she saw him, and I wasn't having that shit. No man on this planet would instill that type of fear in or have that type of power over my woman.

Breelyn told me about the threat he made when she ran into him at the mall, and I knew it had been on her mind heavy. Also, she had been receiving calls on her cell phone where the person would just hold the phone and not say anything when she answered. Then the fact that I spotted someone following us not too long ago really had me thinking ol' boy was up to something. We had no proof it was David, but we definitely had our suspicions. I had Mouse, a tech guy I used from time to time, working on tracing the calls for me.

In the meantime, taking her to the gun range and giving her boxing lessons was what we did for fun. She was leery of handling a gun at first, but now it was second nature. My girl loved that fucking boxing, though, and she got the hang of it in no time at all. She stayed catching a nigga with them combinations I taught her. Her reaction when she saw that nigga let me know that, despite our training, she still wasn't as confident with her newfound skills as I thought she was. I was gon' fix that, though.

It may have seemed fucked up, but I was placing her in a situation to be confronted by the nigga to see how she managed. I watched him watch her from downstairs, so I knew he was going to go after her. Sure, it wouldn't be shit for me to take care of him, but she was used to folks coming to her rescue. I wanted to make sure he knew that he wouldn't be able to intimidate my baby and possibly send her back into hiding. Wasn't trying to change her, but I wanted to make sure she could take care of herself if I wasn't around. I called her "scary ass" a lot, but I didn't think that was her problem at all. She was just a nonconfrontational person. I cherished her sweet nature, but when mu'fuckas came at her, I wanted her to be just as savage as she was with that bitch Jada. Breelyn couldn't stand her and didn't mind letting her know it. I would protect her with my life and wouldn't hesitate to put down any nigga who came for her, but I needed her to be able to stand on her own, as well.

When we first reconnected, I noticed that Breelyn's entire family shielded her from certain things and people, not really allowing her to fight her own battles. That was confirmed by how fast Dakota made it to my place after receiving the text from her saying that she was in trouble. Not long after, her brother was showing up ready to handle whatever problem she had run into. I had no doubt that her whole big-ass family would have shown up too, had they known what was up.

I didn't know what it was, but I just felt like something bad was coming our way, and I would feel better if she was prepared. Things had been going well between us, but I just felt something lurking in the shadows.

When she made it to the blinking red sign that led to the restrooms, my baby glanced my way to make sure I was where she'd left me. I put my phone to my ear to make it seem like I wasn't really paying attention. As soon as she disappeared from my view, I waited, and on cue, that bitch nigga made his way in that same direction.

Chapter 18

Breelyn

Back up off Me

Once inside the restroom, I stepped into the stall to handle my business as gossiping women moved in and out of the luxurious space. Giannis had outdone himself with this place. It was beautifully decorated all the way down to the fancy toilet-paper holders. Once I was done, I moved to the sink to wash my hands. As I touched up my makeup, I felt eyes on me, and I looked in the mirror to see Jada staring at me with that fake-ass smile I hated so much.

"This bitch," I mumbled.

"I don't know what your problem is with me, but I'm not gon' be too many more bitches," she spat with her arms folded across them lopsided-ass titties of hers.

Guessed this ho called herself checking me. She would wait until Kota was nowhere in sight to try coming for me. Bitch was just showing how weak she was. Little did she know, I was no punk and would whoop her ass just as quick as my cousin would. Just because I avoided conflict most times in no way meant that I didn't have hands. I mean I had Elijah Raheem as a big brother and Dakota Layne as my cousin, and my nigga was a fucking paid killer who made sure that I could handle myself. Not to mention the rest of my family was fucking crazy. I was just different from my man, my brother, and Kota. Those muthafuckas went out looking for trouble, just wishing someone would step to them wrong, whereas I preferred to handle shit when provoked.

Except for when it came to this friendly pussy bitch standing beside me. Ain't liked her ass since we were teenagers. At first, it was just because of how close she was with Kota. I was just on some childish, petty shit in the beginning. When she started fucking my brother, my hate for her became real. She was the biggest ho ever, and my brother just wouldn't stop messing with her ass despite warnings from me and Kota about the shit she was doing behind his back. Rah just didn't give a damn. The final straw was when she tried Dakota's ex. Your best friend's man? Really, bitch? Don't get more trifling than that. I was done after that and let her know every time I saw her that I didn't fool with her kind.

"You gon' be as many bitches as I want you to be. Now, what you gon' do about it?" I said, getting in her face. She was always trying to act like shit was sweet when she stayed doing the most. I'd just seen her skinning and grinning in my ex's face when we all knew she used to try throwing the coochie at his first cousin. Like, why was she shocked that people didn't fuck with her?

"I'm just saying I've never done anything to you, but you stay coming for me," she backtracked immediately.

"You fucked over my cousin, so that's just like doing something to me. She don't fuck with you, and neither do I. And yeah, my auntie told me about you coming around asking questions about Rah, too. Whatever little plan you got to sink your claws into my brother again need to be forgotten. That shit ain't ever gon' happen. I know a lot more about your ass than you think I do, so for your own good, you better back the fuck up off of me and anyone else in my family," I said before closing my clutch and exiting the restroom. Everyone was used to chill, laid-back

Breelyn, but I was tired of letting folks run over me. Was thinking I needed to apply that same attitude and thinking when it came to David's janky ass. And, speaking of the damn devil, I ran smack into him when I hit the hallway. I nervously looked around for Rio but didn't see him anywhere.

"Just the person I was hoping to see. You look beautiful tonight, baby girl," David said, tracing his fingertip down the front of my dress between my breasts, which made my skin crawl.

"Get your fucking hands off of me, David. My man wouldn't appreciate you touching what belongs to him," I said, slapping his hand away. Him feeling me up like he had every right to pissed me off.

"Your man? You done lost your damn mind if you think it's going down like that. That bitch Dakota got you acting like you don't have a lick of damn sense," he growled while backing me into the corner away from the entrances to the restrooms. As soon as we were out of view, Jada walked out and went about her business.

"Dakota has nothing to do with me deciding to move on with my life, David. You stay blaming her for shit when it's really all your fault that we're in this place right now. What is your obsession with my cousin?" I countered. Didn't know what it was about Dakota, but he hated her and felt like she wanted to come between us. In actuality, it was his dog-ass ways that caused us to drift apart.

"Man, I ain't trying to hear all that! I'm 'bout sick of this shit, Bree. You been gone long enough. I'm sorry for how shit went down with us, and I also understand why you left me. I realize I should have treated you better. I'm gon' do right this time, baby, I promise. It's time for you to come home now. The only man for you is me, and you know that shit," he stated pitifully.

"David, me and you can't happen, ever," I said with confidence. There was a time when him confessing his wrongs and asking me to come home would have meant the world to me, but now it was too little, too late.

"Why not, bae?" he asked, looking into my eyes. He was desperate for me, but I couldn't fuck with it in no way, shape, or form.

"Because I'm in a relationship with someone else and I'm deeply in love with him," I said, being honest with him. The pain and rage in his eyes caused me to almost take those words back. There was no need, though, because my heart was with DeMario Taylor and that's just what it was. I refused to let him scare me into giving him false hope.

"Bitch, what the fuck did you just say?" he asked through gritted teeth.

He advanced on me, pressing his left forearm across my throat and pushing me hard into the wall. So hard that I was now barely standing on my tiptoes. Can y'all believe that in this moment I wasn't afraid? Like, at all. I was more pissed off than anything. This muthafucka had the balls to put his hands on me because I was with someone else, but he had done more to hurt me than anyone else ever could. I had someone in my life who loved me unconditionally and only wanted the best for me. Someone who didn't do shit to hurt me just for the fuck of it or to see how much I would put up with from him.

I was mad as hell at this point, and the nigga was so busy talking shit that he didn't notice the blade I'd pulled from my clutch. He damn sure felt it when it penetrated his side, though. I purposely didn't cut him deep enough to cause any real damage but just enough to make a point. The pressure he had on my neck lessened and his eyes grew wide in shock before I landed a hard left hook across his jaw.

"Argh!" he yelled out.

With one hand at his side and the other holding his jaw, he looked at me in complete disbelief. My face remained stoic, and I hoped he saw that I was done playing with his ass and there wasn't an ounce of love left for him in me. I never fought back when he beat me, so I was sure this nigga was tripping off the fact that I stuck his ass let alone busted him in his shit. I poked his ass just where my baby had taught me. In a spot that would get him the fuck up off me but not be life-threatening. Just needed him to know that he wasn't going to keep playing with me. Surely had no business putting his hands on me.

The clicking sound of a gun caused him to turn toward the sound. With him turning I was able to see Rio, and I smiled despite the situation I was in. Just seeing his face calmed and comforted me in a way I couldn't begin to explain. Even with the gun pointed toward a man who at one point I would have given my life for, I was unbothered.

"Nigga, you just signed your death certificate fucking with what's mine," Rio said calmly like a crazy person would. "Breelyn, come here, baby," my man instructed me, and I did just that. David looked like he wanted to grab me but thought better of it. His focus was on the gun Rio was holding.

"I'on know why y'all ho-ass niggas thought it was cool to even show up here tonight," Rah added as Giannis came up beside him, both sporting matching mean mugs.

"Breelyn, go upstairs with the ladies, and I'll be there in a minute," Rio instructed before kissing my cheek. "I'm proud of you, baby," he said against my face, earning a small smile from me.

His words and touch were all I needed to put my mind at ease. I didn't bother looking back at David, but I could feel him staring a hole through me. I had no clue what they had planned for his ass, and at this point, I didn't care. Even my brother looked on with pride as I made my way up the corridor.

"Let me find out yo' ass 'bout that life, Greedy," he teased.

"Hush up, Elijah," I laughed and kept it moving.

"Jada and that tacky nigga he came with must have left already. My people can't find them anywhere in the building," I heard Giannis say before I was out of earshot.

When I made it back to VIP, I wasted no time telling the girls about my encounter with David as well as the words I exchanged with Jada in the restroom. Of course, Kota was on ten, wishing she had been there to put Jada in her place, but I told her that I took care of it. I could handle myself, and I wanted my cousin to fall back. I didn't need her fighting my battles for me anymore.

"You know they about to fuck him up, right? If Montell were still here, his ass would be getting dealt with too," Dakota said like it wasn't shit. It was like he never existed or meant anything to her. I guessed her being as in love with Giannis as she was made her realize that what she and Montell shared really wasn't as deep as she thought. I could definitely relate.

"I already know," I told her. The fear I once had for David was gone, and I felt a confidence that I hadn't felt in a very long time. Whatever happened to David tonight, he brought upon himself, and hopefully, it would be enough for him to forget about me and what we had.

Chapter 19

Giannis

Don't Flex, Baby

When I tell y'all I was too fucking hype when Dakota and I made it back to the house, I mean that shit. Baby had already topped me off in the car on our way here, so I already knew tonight was going to be one for the record books.

After hitting up my managers to check in on my spots, I opted to shower in the guest room bathroom while she showered in the master bath. Now I was laid up in bed, waiting on my lady. Kota stepped out after her shower, looking like a Nubian queen, and the look in her eyes told me exactly how tonight was going to go. It told me that nothing about the session that was about to pop off in my spacious bedroom was going to be gentle. No romance. The room was devoid of candles, rose petals, or the usual sandalwood incense. Even the music blasting from the Beats pill assured me that there would be no lovemaking this evening. My baby was about to fuck the shit out of me, and I planned to fuck her fine ass right back.

When I was finally able to tear my gaze away from the skimpy lingerie she was wearing and our eyes connected, I felt the same shit I felt when I saw her at her parents' home all those months ago. That "I have to have her" feeling. At the mere thought of sliding in and out of her pussy, my shit was trying to burst through the Polo boxer briefs I was wearing. Dakota Layne was fine as hell, and I couldn't wait to drop this dick off in her. When her ass started dancing, I sat up in bed with my eyes bucked so as not to miss a single part of her show. Shit!

Don't flex, baby.

I want to see you toucha toes in that dress, baby.

She did exactly what the song said, giving me a perfect view of that ass from behind as it bounced and clapped to the beat.

Bounce it up and down like we having sex, baby.

That part too! Squatting down, legs spread wide, with her hands on her knees as she bounced up and down much like she would do on my dick. Baby twerked and danced while I watched with my mouth hanging open. Might have even just wiped some drool from my chin but whatever. First time she'd ever put on a show like this for ya boy, and I was mesmerized and stuck in a damn trance. If I had known that she had this planned I would have had some cash ready to make it rain on her bad ass.

As it was, I grabbed the small knot from the bedside table and made it rain on her. That would have to do for now, but not even this chump change was enough for the way her oiled-up body moved, swayed, and bounced to the beat of the throwback joint. Although fine as fuck and talented as hell, the females up in Sensations didn't have shit on my girl right now. Her dedication to the gym had her body tight as fuck, and since we started having sex, I noticed her small hips had begun to spread, giving her the perfect silhouette.

My Gawd, I didn't know how much more of this shit I was going to be able to stand before I snatched her ass up and got to it. Right when I was about to make my move, she removed the red lace top from her upper body and tossed it to the side. Wearing nothing but the G-string, which basically consisted of strings attached to a small patch of material covering her sex, she climbed onto the bed, crawling over to me.

"Swear I was about to come grab yo' ass if you hadn't come to me right then," I said seriously, wrapping my arms tightly around her waist as she straddled me. Her super-soaking ass had created a huge wet spot on the front of my boxers just that fast. I wanted so badly to suck on that pussy, but I would have to get a couple nuts off first. I always took care of my baby, so she would have to forgive me for skipping the foreplay just this one time.

"I'm already knowing. I could see it in your eyes," she said before kissing me with nothing but aggressive passion.

"Fuck!" I groaned. The heat radiating from her pussy made my dick grow and harden even more. "Kota, baby, stop playing. My dick so hard this shit hurt," I said against her neck as I licked and sucked on her flesh. Baby rose up to quickly relieve me of my boxers and place me at her entrance before slamming her body down hard on my dick.

"Ahhh!" I called out as she hissed in pleasurable pain. Her shit was so damn tight and wet that my weak ass was about to cum already. Dakota was handling the fuck out of me right now, and I wasn't sure I would be able to let it go down like that. I knew this show was her way of thanking me for tonight, so I would let her do her thing for now. As soon as she ran out of gas, I was gon' serve up that dope dick that she loved so much.

The following day I woke up unsure of where the hell I was. When my eyes finally adjusted to the light shining through the blinds and I became aware of my surroundings, I realized I was in my bed. A nigga didn't even drink much last night, but I felt like I had a damn hangover. Kota had me laid out with a love hangover 'round this bitch, and I wasn't even tripping.

Looking to her side of the bed, I noticed it was empty. She'd been gone for a while, because I remembered losing the warmth that was pressed up against my side when she moved, but I was so tired I couldn't wake up at the time. Flashbacks of our sex session last night played in my mind, causing a wide grin to take over my face. Dakota showed her black ass last night, and with all the nasty shit we did I planned to take these sheets directly to the laundry room. I would have done it last night, but a nigga passed the hell out after that last explosive nut.

"What you in here smiling about?"

Hearing the smile in her voice, I turned my head to see Dakota making her way to me. Seeing her bright smile caused one that rivaled hers to grace my face. This girl just got more beautiful to me every day. Dressed in gray sweats and a black tank with her hair braided in two French braids, she could easily pass for a teenage girl. Makeup free with her face clear and shining like it did every morning, my baby looked like an angel. Nothing about how she looked right now told of the freak shit she was into.

Had never been a fan of anal penetration before last night, but I could honestly say I was down with the movement now. Only with Kota, though. A few homeboys of mine told me how good it was and how their women would go crazy and cum harder from it, but it just wasn't something I really thought was for me. Was a little reluctant when Kota asked for it, but I would do almost anything to please her, so I was like fuck it. There was nothing like being in her pussy, but the way she came when I stuck my lubricated thumb in her ass as I drilled her from behind had me changing my mind real quick. When I replaced my thumb with the dick, her ass was cumming and squirting all over the place, boosting a nigga's ego like a mutha.

"Just reminiscing on last night. Yo' li'l ass was on ten, baby," I laughed as she joined in.

"You had me turned on tough. I couldn't help myself. Get up and shower and I'll take care of this bed linen. I have breakfast waiting for you downstairs," she said while placing kisses all over my face.

"Damn, a nigga get breakfast, too?" I smirked cockily. It was more like lunch since it was well after one p.m.

"You can get whatever you like, baby," she moaned when I fisted her ass.

"I plan to cash in on that promise as soon as I wash my nuts and get some nourishment, so remember you said that," I said on my way to my master bath.

"I got you, honey."

For a moment, I stood in the doorway watching her remove the sheets, thinking how lucky I was to have her in my life. Couldn't wait to make her my wife one day, and the thought of her having my babies had a nigga's heart swelling. A baby girl with Kota's face would surely make this world a better place. Her back was to me, but she felt me staring at her.

"Go on, Giannis. If you keep looking at me like that we'll never leave this room," she said, finally turning to face me biting down on that bottom lip.

"Thank you, Dakota."

"For what, baby?" she asked with one eyebrow raised in confusion.

"For giving me a chance. For letting me love you, and for loving me the way you do. I need you to know that you mean everything to me. I plan to spend the rest of my life proving to you that you made the right decision being with me. I love you, Dakota Layne," I said sincerely. Tears were sliding down her face before I even completed my declaration of love. Ol' sappy ass. "I ain't trying to make you cry, love. Just wanted to tell you how I feel," I comforted her, pulling her into my arms.

With her head still buried in my chest, she spoke. "I know, Giannis, but I just love you so much, and when you say shit like that it makes me emotional. Breelyn already talking about taking my G card and shit. Saying I'm getting soft fucking with you. Now that I'm chilling, she walking around stabbing folk," she chuckled through her tears.

I couldn't do shit but laugh, because Breelyn had suddenly turned into a bad ass. I believed she always had it in her but chose to suppress it for whatever reason. With a nigga like Rio leading her, she had no choice but to become a savage. Hell, I thought Rah's ass was crazy. That nigga Rio had been on a murking spree since he touched down in Texas. The man played no games.

Breelyn was dead-on with what she said about Dakota, though. Even I noticed her becoming softer. More submissive. Less aggressive and gangster. She would still get it popping if need be, but she normally just followed my lead and let me handle shit. Like after I stepped to that nigga Montell the night before. Normally she would have busted him in his shit or told me to let her deal with him, but instead, she took the back seat and let me do me. I needed that from my woman, and I thought I was what she needed in her life all along. A man strong enough to tame her and give her the love she deserved. That other nigga couldn't do that, but a man like me was made for the job.

"Thank you, Giannis. For recognizing my worth. For seeing what I wasn't trying to see in the beginning. For allowing me to love you. And definitely for loving me the way you do. Lord knows no one can do it better."

The vulnerability I saw in her misty eyes had me weak in the knees, and like I always said, I had to have her. "Come shower with me?" I asked as I bit down hard on her shoulder. I knew she'd already handled her hygiene this morning, but I was ready to slide inside one more time. I needed to wash my ass first, though, and I wanted her in there with me.

"Let me get these sheets in the wash, and I'll be right there," she said after a few pecks to my lips.

After joining me in the shower, me and my baby went two more rounds before she served me a breakfast in bed that was fit for a king. That was another thing I loved about her. She could cook her ass off just like the rest of the women in her family, and my ass was fat-fat full when it was all said and done.

For the remainder of the day, we were on some Netflix and chill shit, making love off and on. Swore I never wanted this shit to end. I was focused on the present, because I could feel some crazy shit on the horizon with this nigga David. I didn't like how he kept mentioning Kota's name as he ranted and raved when we were whipping his ass. Rah and Rio were ready to do him in right then, but I talked some sense into them. I knew it wouldn't be long before his time came, though, and I only hoped I wouldn't end up regretting letting him make it last night. Until shit hit the fan, I would continue to run my businesses, stack my bread, and enjoy times like these with my future wife.

Chapter 20

Montell

Getting It Together

Over the last few months, things in my life had taken a turn, and finally it was for the better. At this point, it was about trying to do better for myself and my kids. In the beginning, all I could focus on was trying to earn back Dakota's love and trust, but I thought that ship had officially sailed. Seeing her with someone else at her book release party last weekend had been a wake-up call for me. It was really over, and I had no choice but to accept that. Baby girl seemed happier than I'd ever seen her, and as painful as it was for me to admit it, Dakota deserved that. Of course, I still loved her, but it was time to let go and turn my focus on me and mine.

Thanks to a hookup from my baby mama Erica, I was working and had been for some time. One afternoon when I was visiting li'l Tell, I vented to Erica about not being able to find a job with my background. She saw how determined I was, so she made a call to her mother, who was a supervisor at a temp agency. Mrs. Simmons put me in contact with places that accepted people with felonies on their records. I guessed she never put me on before because she knew I wouldn't keep whatever job her mother was able to find for me, but Dakota leaving me forced me to get my shit together.

Because I was employed and my mother could see the changes I was trying to make, she allowed me to come back to her home until I got on my feet. I was a grown-ass man, so I knew it wasn't cool for me to be there very long. Shouldn't have had my ass laid up with anyone, but I was planning to do better. I was grateful to be staying with my mom, though, because if I had to spend one more second at Ayesha's crib, I knew I was bound to go back to jail. That bitch there was crazy as fuck, and I was making plans to get my daughter away from her the first chance I got. I was working my ass off, saving every dime that I didn't give to my baby mamas and my mother. I was so thankful to have at least one sane baby mama.

One thing I was conflicted about was the feelings I was growing for Erica. Didn't know if it was because Kota wasn't fucking with me or the fact that I hadn't had no pussy in a minute, but something was surely happening there. I always had feelings for her, but lately they had become stronger, and I didn't know what to do about it. Swore I wanted Kota with everything in me, but something deeper was pulling me toward Erica.

She wasn't doing anything spectacular to make it happen, either. She was just being her normal sweet and caring self, and I was becoming attached to her. Found myself sharing bits and pieces of my childhood with her. I didn't go into too much detail, but she was aware that there was some sexual abuse from my alcoholic aunt. Not even Dakota knew about that shit, but I felt comfortable confiding in Erica for some reason.

Despite my shortcomings, I felt like a man when I was with her. She stayed encouraging me, and she treated me like I was someone special. Dakota was supportive when we were together, but after trying to get me to do right and telling me the same shit for years with no action on my part, her delivery became fucked up. She began nagging a lot and tossing out ultimatums if I didn't get my shit together. It was my fault that she had turned into that person, but that constant bitching didn't make shit easier on me. I pushed her to that point, though, so I couldn't even be upset.

Erica was the way Kota was when we first hooked up. Even when I showed up to Erica's place with my daughter, she welcomed us both with open arms. Sometimes she even played with my baby and loved on her while I tended to and spent time with my junior. She basically treated my daughter as if she were her own. If I even mentioned my son around Ayesha's loony ass, a fight was sure to break out. That girl was hateful as hell, and I wouldn't dare bring my boy around her. I would have to end her life if she did anything to harm my child. Either one of them. I was a fuckup, but that didn't take away from the fact that I loved the hell out of my children and I wanted to do better for them.

That's something Kota always pressed me about, and now I finally understood what she'd been trying to drill into my thick head. I didn't want them to grow up not feeling loved or be subjected to abuse like I was. At the moment, I couldn't do a whole lot for them financially, but I was hoping that would change soon. The only things I had were my love and time, and I was determined to give them that much at least.

It was Friday night, and I had just gotten off work. As I pulled up to Ayesha's spot, I said a silent prayer that I could grab my daughter and not have to argue with this girl like I did every weekend. I hated for my daughter to witness the constant bickering, but her mother had no chill whatsoever and an uncanny ability to push my buttons like no other. This, in turn, caused me to entertain her bullshit from time to time instead of just walking away. Tonight I was tired and not in the mood. My mother wanted her grandkids for the weekend, so I prayed again that this pickup went smooth.

From outside the door, I could hear the music blasting and female voices cackling and getting ready for the turn up. It was the same thing they did every weekend, so I was used to it. It took about five minutes before my knocks on the door were answered, and I was becoming more heated by the second.

"Umph," Ayesha grunted when she finally opened the door for me.

"Hey, how you doing, Esha? My baby girl ready?" I asked, trying to be polite despite how I was really feeling. Hopefully, she didn't notice the throbbing vein at my temple, because me getting upset was exactly what she wanted, and I refused to give her ass the satisfaction.

"No, but you know where her shit is, so get her ready yourself," she snapped before taking her seat at the table so that her homegirl, Lexi, could finish curling her stiff-ass purple weave.

Taking a deep breath, I made my way to the back without further comment. She was just aching for me to go off, but it wasn't happening tonight. Ayesha was always trying to show out in front of those bitches she called her friends. Little did she know that two of the three of them who sat in there snickering and tee-heeing had thrown the pussy at me, and on numerous occasions, I'd gladly caught it from both of them. Only after seeing what a bitch Ayesha was did I decide to give in after they had made multiple passes at me.

All I wanted was to get my babies home, then shower and go check on David. We made the wrong move by going to Kota's event the past weekend. It was his idea to fall through, and I wished I had followed my first mind and stayed home. The nigga saying our night was on him was the only thing that got me up out of the bed. Fuck what you heard. When I told y'all I was saving every dime, that's exactly what I meant. I needed a spot big enough for me and my babies for when they came over to spend time with me, so blowing my money at the club was out of the question.

Bet David wished he stayed his ass at home too. Ass ended up getting stabbed by Breelyn and his ass beaten by her new nigga, her brother, and Kota's man. I hated that I left him to face that shit on his own, but I was distraught after seeing Kota with that nigga. Swore I wasted no time getting up out of there. That was my cousin, so we both would have just been beaten the fuck up had I stuck around. Thing was, I didn't think that ass whooping did him any good, because he'd still been on my jack, talking about getting Breelyn to talk to him even after being warned that the next time he came at her, he would be taken completely off the set. Nigga was dumb as fuck if you asked me, but he was family, so I had his back.

Walking into my daughter's room and removing the blanket from her body had all that Mr. Nice Guy shit getting tossed straight out the fucking window. She was fast asleep in bed, wearing dirty clothing, while the room itself reeked of urine. Montelaysia was four years old but still had accidents from time to time, and it seemed that her mother didn't bother to change the sheets or get rid of the soiled clothing, because the room was funky as hell. My baby girl was funky as hell too.

"Esha!" I yelled as I made my way into the bathroom to bathe my daughter, who I'd woken up. This stupid bitch was already teaching Laysia that bad hygiene was okay by doing nasty shit like this.

"The fuck you yelling for, nigga?" she asked with an attitude as she stood her "built Ford tough" ass in the doorway.

"I'm just trying to figure out why my baby in there lying in piss while you play with yo' rat-ass friends! If you was handling your business, she wouldn't still be pissing in the bed, Ayesha!" I argued. I had no clue that this bitch was this fucking trifling, and this shit here gave me the extra push I needed to get full custody of my child. I wouldn't dare go back to the streets, because I wasn't built for it and would surely end up back in jail, but I had to do something. A second job didn't sound too bad right about now. Anything to get my daughter up out of these deplorable conditions.

"Don't come up in here acting like you better than me, nigga. If you was still here with us, maybe she wouldn't be pissing in the bed. She probably misses her father, but no, you had to run back to yo' mama instead of staying here with your family," she said as if her feelings were actually hurt.

"Go 'head with that shit, Esha. You know damn well why I ain't here with y'all, and I spend plenty of time with my daughter. She knows who I am and she knows that I love her," I said, looking into my daughter's pretty eyes.

She offered me a smile, letting me know that she understood what I was saying. My baby knew I loved her because I told her all the time. It was her mother I could do without.

"All that fussing and fighting around my baby is the reason I'm at my T-lady crib, but pretty soon I'll have my own spot so my children can spend even more time with me," I informed her. Her expression quickly went from sorrowful to angry. I couldn't figure her out for shit. When I was here with her and Montelaysia, she treated me like shit, wouldn't fuck me, and didn't take very good care of our child. Now that I was gone, she was in her feelings. Maybe she thought life with me was going to be like how it was with me and Kota, and that just wasn't happening. Mainly because my old life was financed by Dakota and also because I didn't want that life with her. I only came to stay with her because Kota put me out and I had no other choice. Shit was fucked up, but it was true.

"Just take her and get the fuck out of my house, Montell. I hate yo' black ass," she shouted before rushing away in tears. Seconds later I heard her bedroom door slam.

"I love you, baby girl," I told my daughter once I saw tears clouding her pretty, brown eyes.

"I love you too, Daddy." She wrapped her arms around my neck once I had the towel secured around her. I was definitely getting that second job. Had to get my child up out of here soon.

Chapter 21

David

Delusional

"Bitch, if you don't take this dry-ass bullshit back in there . . . Where the fuckin' gravy at and why the fuck you ain't fry it? Always tryin'a bake some shit wit'cho lame ass," I spat at Shawna, who quickly picked up the plate of chicken and rice and took it back to the kitchen without a word.

Her ass knew better than to say something back to me. Looking like she was about to cry as usual. I treated her so badly, because in my mind she was the root of all of my problems. Should have never brought her ass up in the home I shared with my girl in the first place. Now I had to sit here pissed off and hungry as fuck. A nigga was eating good when Breelyn was here, but nowadays I stayed eating out because this ho couldn't cook for shit. At least not food that I liked to eat.

Been sitting over here going crazy all week knowing that Breelyn was actually in a relationship with another man. She was probably catering to him and fucking him the same way she used to do me. I was completely losing my mind behind that shit. Face was busted the fuck up, just really able to see clearly today because my shit had been closed up for days. Three cracked ribs, multiple bumps and bruises, and a wound to my left flank where my baby stabbed me. It wasn't even her character to be violent like that. Must have been some shit Dakota's ratchet ass taught her.

Breelyn was clearly being influenced by all these outside people and wasn't able to think for herself. If she were, she would have been come home already. I knew that if I had the chance to talk to her one-on-one, she would see that with me was where she needed to be. I was even willing to forgive her for fucking with that crazy nigga who wanted to kill me behind that building. Rah was down with it too, but I wasn't surprised because his mental ass never liked me.

Thankfully, that light-skinned nigga came through for me, explaining how a lot of folk saw me in the building tonight and if I came up missing or dead it would most likely lead back to them. Nigga said all that before he commenced beating me with the butt of his gun and warning me to stay away from Breelyn and Dakota. Her so-called man threatened to chop my limbs off one by one if I came anywhere near her again. How my sweet girl ended up with that nutcase was a mystery to me.

I was sitting there thinking of ways to get my baby to meet up with me when the doorbell sounded off. "Bitch, if you don't come get this do', I'ma snap yo' neck," I shouted when I didn't see Shawna making her way to the front to answer the door. Knew she ain't expected me to get up. I really hated speaking to her that way, but it seemed like she got dumber every fucking day. Was glad Davy wasn't here to witness me get on her ass. She just didn't know how many ass whippings my son saved her from on the regular.

"Hey, Tell. He's in the den," I heard Shawna mumble seconds before Montell made his way to the back, where I was propped up with my bottle of Jose Cuervo tequila and different bottles of prescription pills. The hood doctor hooked me

up with Percocet, hydrocodone, and some MS
Contin. Since the day I was beaten I'd been pill
popping and drinking like a fucking fish, sitting
in this exact same spot.

"How you feeling, big cuz?" he said, dappin'
me up.

"Getting better er'day," I lied.

"Better? Nigga, it look like you ain't moved
from this recliner since I was here a few days
ago. Same clothes and everything, so I know you
ain't washed yo' ass. What's really going on with
you, Dave? Aside from them fools coming at you,
it's some mo' shit up with you," he pressed.

"Chill out, Dr. Phil. Ain't shit else going on. Still
missing my girl, but that's about it." I shrugged.

"What about the coke, David? You can lie to a
lot of folk, but I know yo' ass better than anyone,
so let me stop you before you get started," he
said with his hand out toward me.

I was about to lie, but like he said he knew
me better than anyone. I could always keep it
real with him without judgment. "I'ma keep it a
buck with you, cuz. I was on that shit heavy for
a long-ass time. Got even worse when Breelyn
walked out on my ass, but I been clean for a
couple months."

That much was true. I hadn't snorted anything since I got my ass clowned by Breelyn

and Dakota in the mall. The only issue was I'd exchanged one problem for two more. I was already drinking heavily prior to my run-in with them niggas at the lounge. Add in the pills that I could get with no problem from my doctor, and I was quickly becoming addicted. I would keep that part to myself, though. I needed something to cope with the loss I was feeling with Breelyn no longer in my life. I mean she been gone for a minute, but to know she never planned to return was crushing.

"That's good, bruh. That wasn't a good look for you. Know yo' ass too playa to be a fucking junky," he said, dapping me up.

"You already know," I agreed. "I forgot to ask what happened when you and ol' girl left the spot that night."

"Jada?"

I nodded.

"Not a damn thing! I asked for a ride. She dropped me off and dipped. Nothing more. Ever since I told Kota how she tried to give me the pussy that time, she keeps her distance and has never tried me again. She was telling me how Bree confronted her in the restroom, though."

"I don't know what's gotten into her, but she tripped out when she stuck me. That shit has Dakota's name written all over it," I spat.

"How you figure? She probably just tired of you fucking with her," he laughed, pissing me off.

"You always taking up for that ho. Breelyn only jump stupid when Kota's ass is around. All of that back talking and disrespectful shit that Kota does done finally rubbed off on my baby. You should have put that bitch in her place a long time ago, and maybe I wouldn't be dealing with this shit right now. I'ma handle that ass, though."

"Fuck you mean you gon' handle her?" he asked, moving up to the edge of the sofa, mugging me.

"Exactly what I said. What? You still love that bitch or some'n? Her and her nigga clowned your ass, and you worried about what I got planned for her ho ass," I laughed.

"Niggaaa! Yo' ass is delusional as fuck. You the one treated your girl like shit. Cheated. Beat on her. Disrespected her. Same shit I did to Kota. The difference between us is that I own up to my shit and I'm moving on, while your ass still stuck blaming other mu'fuckas for your shitty-ass life. Just because Kota ain't fucking with me don't mean I'm gon' let you do something to her," he challenged.

He was now standing with his fists balled up like he wanted to hit me. Nigga stayed defending that ho, but just like I said, I was gon' deal with that bitch real soon, and then I'd have my girl back with me where she belonged. "Man, sit down, kinfolk. Ain't nobody gon' do shit to your precious Kota. I just have to think of another way to get Breelyn to sit down and talk to me."

"Whatever, man. I'm about to get up out of here. Call me if you need anything," he said before walking out.

I knew Montell was still pissed, but he would get over it. I played that shit off, but I still planned to rid the world of Dakota Bibbs.

Chapter 22

Family Time

Sylvia Bibbs

Today was a damn good day. All my babies came through for Sunday dinner, and I couldn't be happier. Bree and Rah had worked things out and both my girls seemed to be in love and happy with their relationships. They had the family worried for a moment there with those two knuckleheads they were dealing with. *Now if I could just get my nephew to settle down I'd really be pleased.*

Elijah and my daughters' friend don't think folks pick up on the chemistry between the two of them, but I don't miss shit. The looks and unspoken gestures weren't hard to miss, but everyone was so caught up in what they had going on that they're not paying attention. Like I said, Sylvia Bibbs didn't miss a damn thing. They seemed like a good match, but only time would tell.

We were in the den, jumping from topic to topic, and then the conversation somehow switched to marriage and family. Already knowing how my girls felt, I perked up, looking forward to hearing the perspectives of the young men in the room.

"Mrs. Bibbs, how long have you and Mr. Bibbs been together, if you don't mind me asking?" Giannis asked as the family sat crowded in the den watching the Cowboys game. He had my baby girl pulled in close next to him like he was scared she would get away from him somehow. I couldn't help but smile. My girl had finally found her prince after kissing all those low-down, ugly frogs.

"Thirty years together, twenty-eight years married," I answered with a smile. I shuddered a little when I felt my husband give my thigh a caress and squeeze. After all these years just a slight touch from him would have me on edge. Was something special about Kasey Bibbs, honey.

"That's dope. My folks have been together for about the same amount of time. You just don't see relationships like those these days," he said, causing a few old heads in the room to agree.

"That's because a lot of you youngsters too busy hooking up and fucking anything moving instead of trying to build solid, lasting relationships," Herb said, giving his opinion.

"I agree. I always knew that when I found the woman I felt was meant for me, I wouldn't hesitate to lock her down," he said, kissing Dakota's temple softly. "I was raised in a home with both parents. It wasn't easy, but I saw how hard they fought to make things work, and I think that's what's missing from many homes in the black community. Had I not witnessed that growing up, I would more than likely be in the same category of young people that you described. Before I met Kota I was living my life the same way," he admitted.

"As a man raised by a single mother, my thinking is a bit different from G's. Wasn't really focused on finding someone, but I wasn't running from it, either. Let's just say my occupation kept me on the go a lot, and I didn't want to have someone I would have to leave behind or worry about while I was out handling my business. But shit, once I committed to Breelyn, it was nothing for me to scale back on work to make her a priority. I knew I would do whatever I had to do to keep her, protect her, and love her. And that's coming from a man who never knew his father or had any positive male influences in his life. I believe, regardless of the circumstances you grow up in, if it's in you to be a stand-up guy, then that's just what that is. It's a choice," Rio said.

His words made all the women in the room smile widely. Rah, however, sucked his teeth and left the room. My baby was definitely dealing with some shit, and it hurt me that I couldn't help him. Elijah had always been closed off and never liked to discuss his problems with anyone. The only person he would willingly open up to was Kasey. Not even his father could get through to him.

Jada and I stood at the same time. I was going check on him, but I had no clue what she thought she was doing. A nasty look from Breelyn and Kota sat her ass down quick. Didn't know what was going on there, but I was sure I'd find out soon enough. My husband told me to sit back down, and he would go check on his nephew. Breelyn, Dakota, and Mel shared a knowing look while Jada tried playing it off.

Rah

Man, I was in a fucked-up mood and the conversation they were having didn't make it any better. And why did she have to be here today of all days? It was too much being around her ass right now, but I couldn't help staring at her every chance I got. Seemed like her ass was coming around even more since we ended shit, and it pissed me off.

I knew it was crazy, but that's just how seeing her so often made me feel. Hated that I was so into her ass. I knew that besides her one sibling she didn't really have a lot of family, so I felt bad for not wanting her there, but it was hard being around her. Especially when she stayed on the phone, skinning and grinning with some nigga the entire time.

The last time she met up with me at the spot, I fucked her ass all night long, and she gave me one last chance to make things official between us. Once again I turned her down. Just couldn't do it. She was the last person I wanted to hurt, and that's exactly what would happen if I committed to something I wasn't sure I was ready for. She was crushed by my admission but said she understood.

Before she left my place, she made me promise to let her move on and not interfere with her life. Because I couldn't give her what she needed right now, I agreed. I mean, I really ain't have no choice. She was ready for marriage and babies.

The whole nine yards, you know. And by all means, she deserved all that and so much more, but I was scared of not being able to live up to her expectations or failing her in some way. My thoughts alone were scaring the fuck out of me because I'd never considered these things with any other female. Had me wondering if this was what it felt like to be in love. I didn't know, but I needed to talk to someone about this shit before I fucked up and lost the best thing that ever happened to me. I was low-key scared that I'd already missed my chance.

Right on time like always, my Uncle Kasey came to stand beside me at the island in the kitchen. I could always talk to him, and he would never sugarcoat things for me. Always gave it to me raw and real. Was more of a father to me than my biological father, and for that, he would always have my respect. Swore I loved this dude.

Kasey Bibbs

"Nephew, what's up with you?" I asked, knowing he would be real with me if he wasn't with anyone else. It was clear he was having woman problems, because he dipped as soon as the conversation shifted to love and relationships. Never known him to have a girlfriend, but there comes a time in every man's life when the sleeping around just isn't cutting it anymore. Nothing like coming home to someone who loves you and belongs to you and only you. Someone to discuss your day with, cook you food, fuck you good, and keep you warm at night. Nothing like it.

"I'm cool, Uncle Kase. Just tripping off that shit they talking in there. They make it sound so fucking easy, and it's annoying as hell," he said as he downed a shot of moonshine.

"It is easy when you meet the woman who's for you, Rah. You just have to want it and stop trying to avoid it."

"I do want that. At least I think I do." He shrugged.

"You can have that. Hell, you deserve it just like anyone else. What's holding you back, Elijah?" Only called him by his first name when I was serious and wanted his honest answer.

His shoulders slumped, and his head lowered before he answered, "Scared."

"Of?" I asked, fixing myself a shot and another for him.

"Fucking up and having someone I care about walk out on me because of it. I'on even know if I'm capable of loving a female anyway. It's not like I had a good example."

"The fuck you think I been trying to show you all these years, Elijah?" I knew what he was trying to say, but I needed him to really think about the shit that came out of his mouth.

He immediately raised his head to look in my face after realizing his mistake. "I ain't mean it like that, Uncle Kase. Just saying my mama left us too soon, and my pops basically checked out right after. Maybe that's where my real problem lies. You and Auntie Syl been a great example for me and baby sis, but somehow we still fucked up on this relationship shit. At least Greedy got her shit together. Me? I feel like I'm fucking stuck," he said, shaking his head. "Why can't I just be normal like G? Shit, even this nigga baby sis is with got his shit together. He's crazy as hell, but I know he cut for my sister and he does not mind letting the world know it. Even went up against me for her. I would never tell him, but he earned my respect with that."

"Not everybody's situation will be the same, son. Don't look at your sister's and cousin's relationships like you're doing something wrong. You have some things that you need to work out before you commit yourself to another person anyway. You're holding on to shit from the past that had you need to sort out, and you can't continue being afraid to take a chance. The love of the right woman can take care of all those fears. I have a feeling you done already found her and that's the reason you're having the thoughts you're having. I know you, boy, so for us to even be having a conversation about this shit tells me a lot."

He only nodded, and I chuckled. She was the perfect fit for him, but she would have to go through his aunt and sisters to get to him, and I didn't know how easy they would make it for her. I was looking forward to seeing how it all played out.

"Thank you, Unc. Not just for today but for everything."

"It's nothing, son. I got you if no one else does," I told him as we bumped fists then hugged the way men do.

Dakota

I didn't know what this ho Jada was on, but I was extremely close to smacking her ass up. She left before I had a chance to confront her for showing up to my book release party, but I had time today. Why she thought it was cool to still come around was beyond my understanding, but after today I was planning to let her know to stay the fuck away from my family if she didn't want to get her ass beaten.

She used to be one of my closest friends, but the moment she thought it was okay to push up on my nigga was the moment our friendship ceased to exist. Like, she really tried to fuck Montell, and he wasted no time letting me know what went down. When I confronted her, she copped to the shit, talking about she was drunk and not in her right mind, but I wasn't buying it. Montell was a cheater and a whole bunch of other things, but fucking with one of my friends was something I knew he wouldn't do, or so I thought.

A while back, Breelyn told me she learned from David that Montell and Jada had actually fucked and were seeing each other before and after this last time he was locked up. Surprisingly, that bit of information didn't hurt or move me in any way. I shouldn't have put anything past Montell, but I never thought Jada would do me like that. Over the years I accepted her and defended her when everyone talked trash about what a tramp she was. I helped her fight when different females came at her behind fucking with their man. All that and she was fucking my nigga behind my back. She'd been apologizing since then, not knowing that I now knew the real deal between her and Montell. If she burned me once, what would stop her from doing it again? She wouldn't get the chance to try me with Giannis Williams, though. I'd kill that bitch behind that one there. Fuck what you heard.

The fact that she was coming around a lot more than usual had me skeptical. Didn't know if she was plotting on one of our niggas or she was trying to get back in good with Rah, but I was paying close attention to her moves. My mother wasn't aware of what had gone down between us, so she still welcomed Jada and treated her as she always had when she came through. Breelyn never liked her ass, so the two of them shading each other back and forth was nothing new for the family.

I noticed how she was behaving with Rah and I didn't like that shit at all. I wouldn't be surprised if he was still fucking her, but as far as something more developing between them, I wasn't having it, and neither was Breelyn. Bitch was scheming on something, and I was prepared to shut it down before she could even get started.

Breelyn and I had retreated to my old bedroom to talk, and Jada's ass was currently the topic of discussion.

"I still don't like that bitch. Even Rio said something ain't right about her, and you know my baby be knowing," she said with her eyebrows raised. "And why the fuck she keep trying to make conversation with my brother? Touching him and shit with her ol', skank ass," she fumed.

"I don't know, but I'ma get that bitch told today, believe that. My mama too damn nice. She should know that some shit went down with us, seeing as how I don't kick it with Jada no more, but she steady having her over for family shit. And Rah bet' not be checking for that ho. It ain't going down like that."

"Fuck no! I'll stop speaking to that nigga just like he did me," Bree spat seriously, making me laugh.

We were only up there talking for about fifteen minutes before Giannis came up to find me. He didn't like to be away from me for too long, and I was the same way about him.

"Hey, honey," I said.

"Hey, love. I'm about to make a quick run with Rah, but I should be back in an hour or so. We can head home after that," he said before kissing my lips gently.

"Is everything all right?" I asked in between kisses. Didn't think I'd ever tire of having his soft lips on mine.

"Yes, everything is cool," he said before kissing me again. This time a lot deeper. By now Breelyn had become used to our touchy-feely relationship, so she paid us no mind as we tongued each other down.

"Check out the lovebirds," I heard from the door. I looked up to see Jada standing there admiring us with what seemed like a genuine smile.

"Mind yo' fucking business," Bree snapped, surprising Giannis and me. Hell, even Jada was taken aback by her bluntness. Everyone was used to the nice, quiet Breelyn, but that nigga Rio brought the savage out of her. I loved it. She didn't like Jada, and she wasn't going to pretend that she did.

"Damn, what the fuck is your problem?" Jada asked, pretending to be clueless.

"The problem is you bringing your ass around here like shit is sweet. You know damn well I don't fuck with you like that, but you keep popping up," I answered before Bree had the chance. Giannis was so used to me popping off that he kept his arms around my waist and continued kissing my ear and neck as I went in. "Looks like I'm gon' have to tell Moms what went down, so she'll know to turn your loose-pussy ass around at the door the next time you show up," I spat.

"Kota, I thought we were past that. I've apologized over and over, and I assure you that nothing like that will ever happen again," she pleaded.

Bitch actually sounded sincere, but I couldn't fuck with it. "Oh, I know it won't happen again, because I can't rock with you like that no more. And, baby, if you tried to step to this one here, I'd body your ass," I spoke while pointing at Giannis. He simply leaned back and grinned at how possessive I was acting over him. He was usually the one on some shit like this when it came to other niggas coming at me, but it was my turn to cut up behind him.

"Fuck y'all got going on?" Rah asked, entering the tension-filled room. His eyes traveled from an angry Bree to me, then to a sad-faced Jada.

"Nothing. I was just coming to tell the ladies I was leaving." Jada shook her head regretfully. "I really am sorry, Dakota," she added before walking away. Both Breelyn and I chucked deuces and rolled our eyes at her retreat.

"Ol' fake-ass bitch," Breelyn mumbled.

"Man, y'all mean as hell," Rah said, sucking his teeth at us.

"I know you ain't talking with yo' ornery ass," I said.

"I'll be outside waiting on you, bruh. Need to go make sure this girl is straight. Know she probably in the car crying by now," he said, shaking his head at us.

"Why you care, Elijah Raheem?" Bree asked, shooting up to a sitting position on the bed to focus on her brother.

"Yeah, nigga, let me find out," I warned. Swore I was gon' be heated if he was fucking that ho again. I'd been meaning to bring up his relationship with Jada, but I hadn't got around to it. I could have been wrong, but I felt like something was brewing between them. Seeing him snatch her up at the book signing when they thought no one was looking only heightened my suspicions.

"Mind ya business, Kota B," he said with his back to us as he continued down the hall.

"Let's make it, Greedy. I'm ready to go, baby," Rio said loudly as he passed by Rah, who stopped to stare him down for a second before deciding to press on.

That nigga stayed trying to piss Rah off, and it was too funny because Rah fell into his trap 99 percent of the time. My cousin would never admit it, but the two men acted so much alike that it was crazy. It was probably the main reason they couldn't get along.

Chapter 23

Dakota & Breelyn

There's Been a Mix-up

"Baby, did Breelyn pick the car up yet?" I asked with my cell phone, on speaker, face up on my desk. I was at the office for a few hours sorting through and signing some paperwork, so Giannis agreed to stay at the house until my cousin showed up. Her car was down, so she would have my whip for the next few days.

Giannis was basically living with me now and hardly ever went home to his condo. I couldn't wait for it to be permanent because I loved going to sleep and waking up wrapped tight in his arms.

"Not yet, but after she leaves I'm going to step out to get dinner, so don't worry about stopping on your way home," he replied.

"Thank you, bae," I responded. "You know I wasn't trying to stop anywhere." He laughed.

"I already know. I got you, though. And make sure you check your e-mail while you're there. I sent another listing that you need to take a look at."

"Okay. Just let me finish up, and I'll check it out," I replied, shuffling around the papers that were on my desk.

"Cool, see you soon, baby."

"I love you."

"I love you too, Kota B," he said before hanging up.

Goodness, I just loved me some him. It just seemed like everything about him was made just for me and vice versa. No longer did I give a fuck about all the bullshit I had to endure to get to this point. Exes getting married mere months after dumping me, being cheated on, and disrespected in the worst ways possible by someone who claimed to love me. Again, none of that mattered to me as long as it led me right here with this man in my life.

Quickly signing the documents remaining on my desk, I logged into my Gmail account to check out the listing my baby had sent to me. We were currently looking for a home in the Frisco area but hadn't found anything that we both liked. My current home was nice, but Giannis and I wanted to live in a home that we picked out together. I knew it wouldn't be long before marriage and children came into the picture, so we wanted to be prepared and settled before that happened. As much as we got it in, I was surprised I wasn't already knocked up despite being on birth control.

"Damn, this is nice," I said to myself as I flipped through the pictures of the five-bedroom, four-bathroom, two-story home. The property had a pool, which was a must for me. It was huge, yet there was enough yard for entertaining family and friends, which was something the both of us required. Family was number one in both our lives, so it was important for us to have enough space for everyone to mingle and be comfortable while visiting us. The game room, theater, and brand new stainless-steel appliances in the kitchen basically sealed the deal for me. I could use the office downstairs for myself, and we could turn one of the bedrooms upstairs into an office for Giannis. He had a lot of shit popping off with his businesses, so he needed a separate space to organize and manage things. We would need to see it first before making a decision, but in my heart, I felt it was the perfect first home for us, so I quickly shot him a text.

Kota Love: I want it! I want it! It's perfect!

My Honey: Lol. I figured you would like it. We can take a look at it on Monday. Love you.

Kota Love: Love you too.

As I was shutting down my computer, I heard some movement up front. I was here alone this afternoon and had stupidly forgotten to lock the door. Glancing down at my schedule, I saw that I wasn't expecting any appointments, so I had no clue who was walking through the door of my business right now. I wasn't tripping, though, because y'all know I had my .22 sitting on my lap where only I could see it. Not to mention the pepper spray and Taser that sat in my top drawer, which was slightly open for easy access. There ain't a soul alive who could say they caught Kota B slipping and there never would be.

Cool, calm, and collected, I leaned back farther into my plush chair and waited. Ready for whatever. That was, until Montell poked his big-ass head in the doorway. All I could do was lean back and roll my eyes to the ceiling. Hadn't heard a peep from him since the night of my book release and I was happy about that. Figured he'd finally gotten the picture and decided to let go of any thoughts of us being together again. Obviously, I was wrong.

"I see you're already rolling your eyes, so I'll make this quick," he said with his hands out. Guessed he saw me move mine to my lap, and trust he knew exactly what that meant.

"Please do, because I have no idea what we could possibly have to say to one another at this point," I stated calmly.

"I'm not here to cause any problems, so chill," he said, looking down again at my lap before taking a few steps toward the desk.

"Talk, Montell. If I ain't home soon my nigga gon' be up here, and neither you nor I want those problems," I said, being petty.

"Whatever, man. I just came here to talk to you about David," he retorted, clearly bothered by the mention of my man.

"I don't give two fucks about yo' ho-ass cousin. If that's what you're here for, you can leave now. Anything to do with that cokehead nigga, I don't want to hear or have anything to do with it."

"Even if it got something to do with you and your cousin?" he snapped.

"Bree don't fuck with David no more, and I ain't never cared for the nigga so no, I still don't give a fuck," I snapped back.

"I'on mean like that, Kota, damn! I'm saying the nigga been tripping lately talking about doing you and your cousin harm. I went by his spot after that book release shit, and the nigga was still heated about Breelyn being there with that nigga and mad because they whooped his ass. For some reason, he thinks the only reason that Breelyn won't take him back is because of you. Says you have too much influence over her and that if he gets you out of the way she'll come home." He sighed as if telling me this was hard on him.

"I think I'll be okay, Montell, but I do appreciate you coming to tell me this. I know how close you are with Dave," I sympathized.

"Look, Kota, I know you can take care of yourself, but this nigga ain't been in his right mind for a minute. I know you keep your protection on you at all times, but it's deeper than that at this point. Shawna left his ass, and before she skipped town with Davy, she stopped by Mom's and told me all the shit that's been going on over there. Nigga got off the coke, but now he's popping pills and is a full-fledged alcoholic. Said she just couldn't take the beatings anymore or being around him, period. She also told me he was asking around, trying to find someone to kill you, but his broke ass couldn't afford the fee. Now he talking about setting houses on fire and cutting brake lines on your cars."

After hearing that last part, I totally tuned him out as I felt all color drain from my face. My heart was literally racing. I picked up my cell, dialing my man's phone. The phone rang until his voicemail picked up. He must have left the house already to get food and forgotten his phone in the car. I didn't bother leaving a message. Next, I dialed Breelyn and got no answer. This bad feeling suddenly came over me, and I just knew something was wrong. I was up out of my seat, grabbing my belongings and preparing to go see about my cousin. She was probably fine, and the dread I was feeling was due to hearing the plans David had for us. At least that's what I was hoping.

"What else did he tell her?" I asked, suddenly remembering Montell was sitting there.

"She says he was just out of it, rambling on and on about what he was gon' do to you. I tried to call you, but you still got me blocked, and I didn't want to cause problems by stopping by your place. This is actually my second time coming here trying to catch you," he replied, standing when he noticed my panicked state. Was so out of it that I didn't hear another person enter the building.

"Dakota!" I heard Giannis call out, stopping me dead in my tracks.

"Shit!" I mumbled. The last thing I wanted was for him to be under the impression that Montell and I had some other shit going on. From the look in his eyes when he dotted the door of my office, that's exactly what he was thinking.

"The fuck is he doing here, Dakota?" he asked, grilling me hard as fuck.

"Had you answered your phone when I called you, you would have known the answer to that, Giannis," I retorted, immediately jumping on the defensive. That was obviously the wrong move based on the heated look he shot me. I'd done nothing wrong, but I couldn't help but feel he was accusing me of something. My ass had been tripping and hella emotional lately, and he'd called me out several times in the last few weeks.

"Look, man, I ain't here on no bullshit with your lady. I just stopped by to warn her about some shit my cousin was saying he was going to do to her and Breelyn. Nigga been making threats about killing them both and I took it serious enough to at least warn her," Montell spoke up. "I love my cousin, and I feel like shit even being here talking to y'all about him, but I would feel like shit if something happened to her and I had kept this shit to myself. Nigga been wilding since y'all beat his ass that night. I keep telling his ass to let it go but he won't. Talking real reckless about y'all but mostly Dakota. Can't figure out why he hates her so much," Montell said, rubbing his hand down his head in deep thought.

I never told Tell about David trying to get with me before he approached Breelyn or the comments he would make to me when he and Breelyn weren't close by. Giannis knew all about it, because he confronted me the morning after my book release. My honey said that he just knew something was up based on the number of times David mentioned my name that night when Breelyn should have been his main focus. I could see his expression go from angry at me being in here alone with Montell to furious that David was making threats on my life. Right now, arguing was the last thing we needed to be doing.

He came right over and wrapped me up in his arms, because he knew that was what I needed at the moment. Now, making sure that my cousin was straight was my main priority. "Babe, how long ago did Breelyn pick up the car?"

"Maybe twenty minutes ago. Why?" he asked.

"Just something Montell said to me about David threatening to cut the brake lines on my car and burning down houses and shit. I been calling her but she hasn't answered, and I just have a bad feeling," I said, getting worked up.

"That nigga said what?" Giannis's deep voice boomed. He pushed me back to look at my face, and all I could see in his beautiful eyes was pure rage. "You know his ass is dead, right?" he said, turning to Montell, who just looked off, not offering up a response.

I quickly began packing up my shit and dialing Breelyn back to back with no answer. "Baby, you have Rio's number, right?" I asked as I set the alarm and locked up the door to my business. "I remember Breelyn mentioning something about going to spend the weekend with him," I recalled.

"Yeah, let me hit him up real quick." He pulled his phone out, scrolling for the number before sliding his thumb to the right on the device.

"Kota, I'ma head out. I'm sure Bree is fine. Even still, I already know what's up once Rah hears about this shit," he sighed while looking to me with pleading eyes, trying to see if there was anything I could do to spare his cousin's life.

Montell knew better than that. Shit was out of my hands, and even if it were up to me, his ass would still be out of there. I just shook my head, letting him know that I had no sympathy for that nigga. There was nothing that I could do to stop what would happen once Rah was put up on game. Just the fact that the nigga had plans and was actually seeking out someone to kill one or both of us sealed his fate.

Montell knew as well as I did that his cousin was as good as dead. It had to be hard for him to be in the position he was in, though, and I sympathized somewhat. To be torn between doing the right thing or standing by your family and allowing some fuck shit to go down? Talk about a dilemma. I was just glad he made the decision to come here today so that we could at least be aware that we had someone lurking in the shadows who had a problem with us. Shit was wack as fuck if you asked me, but the way men dealt with rejection would forever be a mystery to me. Montell himself displayed some of the same bitch-nigga tendencies as David did when it came to moving on, but thankfully he'd come to his senses. Had he not, he would be on the chopping block right along with his people.

Breelyn

"Okay, baby. All I have to do is stop by the store to pick up the food. Then I'll be on my way out there," I told DeMario through the phone feature in Kota's Audi as I pulled out of her driveway. I had to put my car in the shop yesterday, so she loaned me hers until my baby was ready. Since I had the weekend off, I was spending it with my man at his place. I couldn't wait for our home in Allen to be ready so that I would no longer have to make this drive, but it was worth it just to be able to see and spend time with him. Soon we'd be living under the same roof, and I couldn't wait to have him with me every day.

Although Rio agreed to be the designated chef while I was there, I knew I'd end up cooking most of our meals. I didn't mind, though. I loved cooking, and the fact that he enjoyed my food so much was an added bonus. I planned to stock up on all his favorites so that I could feed and fuck him for the next forty-eight hours. He'd been out of town, and I'd been working like crazy trying to occupy my time while he was gone, so this staycation was just what the doctor ordered.

"Take your time, and I'll see you when you get here. I've been missing you like crazy, so don't be surprised if I pounce on you as soon as you walk through the door."

He laughed, but I knew he was serious, too. We'd been joined at the hip since he came back into my life. This was the first out-of-town job he'd taken since we made things official, so this week without him was terrible. Daddy was back now, so it was about to be on and popping.

"If I don't jump on your ass first," I flirted.

"That's how you feeling, Breelyn?" The smile on his face was evident.

"Hell yeah. I missed you, daddy," I cooed.

"Breelyn, quit playing on this gotdamn phone and come home. Got me rocked up like a mu'fucka talking like that," he groaned. "I'm seriously about to say fuck that food and just take you out to eat all weekend if it will get you here quicker."

"Okay, okay, let me stop. I'm coming up on Kroger right n . . . The fuck!" I panicked when the car wouldn't slow down as I approached the light. I wasn't going more than thirty-five miles per hour, but it was like the breaks were nonexistent right now. I'd noticed a little something when I first got in the car, but I just planned to tell Kota to have it checked out. "Rio, baby, something is going on with the car. Oh my gosh!" I shrieked.

"Breelyn, baby, what's going on?" he shouted. I was too worked up to even respond to his question.

"Shit, shit, shit!" I screamed as the car continued into the intersection. I couldn't stop, and my blaring horn did nothing to alert other drivers that I was having an issue. Fucking Texas drivers! I'd barely turned my head to the right, and a split second later the passenger side of the car was being rammed by an eighteen-wheeler traveling well beyond the speed limit of forty miles per hour. The smashing of metal, glass breaking, and my man's voice calling out to me in a panic was all I heard before everything went black.

To Be Continued